The Mountains
of Parnassus

The Mountains
of Parnassus
Góry Parnasu

Czeslaw Milosz

Translated from the Polish by Stanley Bill

Yale UNIVERSITY PRESS · NEW HAVEN AND LONDON

A MARGELLOS
WORLD REPUBLIC OF LETTERS BOOK

The Margellos World Republic of Letters is dedicated to making literary works from around the globe available in English through translation. It brings to the English-speaking world the work of leading poets, novelists, essayists, philosophers, and playwrights from Europe, Latin America, Africa, Asia, and the Middle East to stimulate international discourse and creative exchange.

Yale University Press books may be purchased in quantity for educational, business, or promotional use. For information, please e-mail sales.press@yale.edu (U.S. office) or sales@yaleup.co.uk (U.K. office).

Set in MT Baskerville type by Tseng Information Systems, Inc.
Printed in the United States of America.

Library of Congress Control Number: 2016937572
ISBN 978-0-300-21425-3 (hardcover : alk. paper)

A catalogue record for this book is available from the British Library.

This paper meets the requirements of ANSI/NISO Z39.48-1992 (Permanence of Paper).

10 9 8 7 6 5 4 3 2 1

Contents

Translator's Introduction
Science Fiction as Scripture

The image of Nobel Prize–winning Polish poet Czeslaw Milosz (1911–2004) as a science fiction writer is strange and incongruous. Even in the context of Poland's highly literary tradition of science fiction writing, it is difficult to imagine this archetypal European intellectual immersing himself in the world of space travel and alien planets. Milosz was a profoundly historical writer, poring over the past in its personal, political, and philosophical dimensions, while science fiction focuses on the future. Milosz identified himself above all as a lyric poet, evincing deep suspicion for the novel as a genre, while science fiction has largely found expression in creative prose. Milosz was a poet of nature, or the "unattainable earth," finding words to capture the idealized landscapes of his native Lithuania or the wilder expanses of later American exile, while science fiction envisions new technologies, cosmic voyages and distant stars. And yet between 1967 and 1971 Milosz worked sporadically, and for brief periods even intensively, on a science fiction novel entitled *The Mountains of Parnassus* (*Góry Parnasu*).[1]

Milosz abandoned the project in March 1971, but initially he seemed determined to do something with the fragments he had already written. From a manuscript of 112 pages, he produced a more streamlined typescript, comprising five edited chapters and an explanatory preface of "Introductory Remarks." In 1972, he sent the typescript to his longtime publisher and supporter, Jerzy Giedroyc, editor in chief of the émigré Polish publishing house Instytut Literacki in France. Giedroyc offered his honest opinion in a letter, describing the work as a "not very successful attempt at a novel," to which Milosz responded: "If you don't like *The Mountains of Parnassus*, then don't print it. In fact, I'd rather you didn't print it. My own attitude to the work remains undetermined."[2]

Whether or not Milosz ever clarified his opinion of his fragmentary novel, he made no further attempt to publish it. He deposited both the manuscript and the typescript in the Beinecke Rare Book and Manuscript Library at Yale University, where—as he wrote in a later poem—he had "decided to dwell when nothing any more / Would be revealed by his ashes."[3] Several years after Milosz's death in 2004, the young Warsaw intellectual Sławomir Sierakowski, founder of the left-wing think tank and publishing house Krytyka Polityczna (Political Critique), stumbled upon the typescript while on a fellowship at Yale, and decided that it deserved to see the light of day, arguing that the work was "unpublished rather than unfinished."[4]

In 2012, Krytyka Polityczna brought out a hardback edition of the novel, with the blessing of the Milosz estate, including an introduction and appendix by Sierakowski, an afterword by the poet's former personal secretary Agnieszka Kosińska, and facsimiles from both the manuscript and typescript. The edition also included "Ephraim's Liturgy," a short text published separately by Milosz in Giedroyc's *Kultura* magazine in 1968, though clearly connected through theme and character to the larger work. Kosińska took editorial responsibility, generally following the typescript and the author's handwritten amendments to it. Given Milosz's towering stature in Polish culture, the posthumous publication of a previously unknown work, even one in fragmentary form, was inevitably a significant event in Poland. All the major daily newspapers and literary magazines published reviews, most of them concurring that the work was not an unqualified artistic success but that it still offered a disturbingly plausible vision of the future decline of Western civilization and valuable insights into Milosz's creative process.

In the Introductory Remarks, Milosz himself begins with an admission of defeat, describing his chapters as "a science fiction novel that will never be written." He gives two main reasons for his failure: first, the novel as a genre has become impossible, since the modern demands of formal experimentation conflict with the original narrative instinct that conceived it; and second, his depiction of the future would be unrelentingly dark, and it is—in his view—immoral for art to oppress people with such bleak visions of human life. These explanations are consistent with arguments that Milosz makes elsewhere about the fate of the novel and the writer's responsibilities to his or her readers, though he also offers a self-deprecating account of his own justifications as "the grimaces of a fox pronouncing that the grapes were sour because they were too high up."

Despite his apparent misgivings, Milosz still went to the considerable trouble of selecting material from the manuscript, typing it out, writing an introduction, and then sending it across the ocean to Jerzy Giedroyc. Clearly he saw something of potential interest to readers in this rough collection of chapters, even if he changed his mind in the wake of Giedroyc's blunt assessment. In fact, it seems that it was precisely in the work's formal looseness that Milosz detected certain intriguing opportunities. He even suggests that he might have "stumbled upon an experimental genre."

In this context, we should note that Milosz was working on *The Mountains of Parnassus* during a period of intense preoccupation with the broader problem of how to liberate literary form from the limitations of the established genres. In 1968, a year after he had commenced work on his abortive science fiction side project, Milosz included a quasi-programmatic statement of this ambitious general intent in an important poem entitled *"Ars poetica?"*:

> I have always aspired to a more spacious form
> that would be free from the claims of poetry or
> prose
> and would let us understand each other without
> exposing
> the author or reader to sublime agonies.[5]

Later, in 1974, three years after abandoning *The Mountains of Parnassus*, Milosz published the long poem *From the Rising of the Sun (Gdzie wschodzi słońce i kędy zapada*), which many critics have regarded as the triumphant realization of his earlier stated aim. This lengthy multipart work includes a mixture of poetry and prose; direct citations from philosophy, literature, family chronicles, folk songs, and conversations; and extracts from legal documents written in the Polish-Belarusian hybrid language of the sixteenth-century Polish-Lithuanian Commonwealth, along with key lines in Lithuanian, French, English, and liturgical Latin. In this self-declared *magnum opus*, Milosz sought to reinvent lyric poetry as polyphony, while still submitting the diverse voices of the poem to the guiding authority of a strong lyric speaker.

We find a less ambitious form of controlled polyphony in *The Mountains of Parnassus*. Indeed, Polish commentators have observed that all the characters seem like versions or aspects of Milosz himself. Karel and Lino Martinez confront existential crises familiar from biographical and autobiographical accounts of Milosz's youth, including a suicidal game of Russian roulette attested by biographer Andrzej Franaszek. Cardinal Vallerg and Ephraim echo many of the older Milosz's views on the decline of Western civilization, and especially on the United States, where the poet was a faculty member at the University of California, Berkeley, for several decades, including the turbulent 1960s. The attentive reader can easily recognize arguments and observations from his contemporaneous collection of essays on America, *Visions from San Francisco Bay* (*Widzenia nad Zatoką San Francisco*, 1969).

Of course, multivoicedness in itself is hardly an innovation in a mid-twentieth-century novel. Instead, the "experimental" activity of *The Mountains of Parnassus* takes place in a peculiar variety of prose lying somewhere on the border between novelistic exposition and essay. The fragments that Milosz prepared for publication detail the characters' backgrounds and the structure of a future world ruled by a totalitarian planetary state, while offering only the vaguest hints of a plot. We know that some kind of religious community in opposition to the ruling Astronauts'

Union has been established in the wilderness of the Parnassus Mountains, but otherwise the chapters present Milosz's predictions of a dystopian future based firmly on the civilizational trajectories he observed in his own time, especially in California. The work is incomplete as a story—in fact, the story never really begins—but perhaps complete as an exercise in speculative world creation.

In the essays of *Visions from San Francisco Bay*, Milosz analyzes the trends as he sees them in contemporary America; in the fictionalized descriptions of *The Mountains of Parnassus* and "Ephraim's Liturgy," he imagines their future consequences. According to his predictions, the increased automation of production will make the vast majority of human beings essentially superfluous, reliant on the prodigious surpluses yielded by advanced technology and left to occupy themselves with trivial amusements. At the same time, the decline of religion and the degeneration of art create a void of meaninglessness that unbridled sex, drug use, and electric current stimulation cannot fill. In this empty world of material feast and spiritual famine, the authoritarian planetary state devises radical measures to deal with increasing numbers of suicides, as people choose death over a life deprived of any higher meaning.

In short, the imaginative extrapolation of a science fiction novel allowed Milosz to extend the temporal field of his social and political reflections from the present into the future. At times, the essayistic discursiveness of the prose slows it down, as the narrator and characters rather unceremoniously dump exposition on the reader. Yet the strongest passages resound with the urgent conviction of prophecy. Indeed, at around the same time, Milosz was directly exploring the potential connections between science fiction and prophecy in an essay entitled "Science Fiction and the Coming of the Antichrist." In this short piece, he even likens science fiction writing to religious scripture, arguing that both genres use the same basic grammatical conceit to make their prognostications of the future more plausible:

> We would include here any narrative that pretends to be written in the past tense, whereas it should have been written in the *futur accompli;* it should have been, but cannot be, because grammar itself stands in the way. . . . A prediction (since we are dealing with predictions) is disguised grammatically: a hero living in the year 3000 "did" and "went." But we find the same thing in the Revelation of St. John: that which is predicted is told as something that has already occurred—in a vision on the island of Patmos.[6]

The essay also reveals the probable influence of Russian theologian Vladimir Solovyov's *Three Conversations* (*Tri razgovory*, 1900) on the development of *The Mountains of Parnassus*. In particular, we should note the similarities between the testament of Cardinal Vallerg and, in *Three Conversations*, a mysterious manuscript supposedly written by a monk named Pansopheus, which Milosz discusses in his essay. Solovyov's monk sets out the dramatic history of the twentieth and twenty-first centuries, tracing a process of religious decline and transformation that shares a great deal with the steady erosion of Christian faith articulated by Milosz's cardinal. On a more metaphysical level, Pansopheus describes the coming of the "Antichrist," while Vallerg refers to a "malevolent presence" growing in force and even becoming a direct object of worship. At certain key moments, the cardinal reveals this presence as the "Prince of This World," or "diabolos"—the Devil.

Admittedly, Cardinal Vallerg's testament is not especially typical of science fiction writing in either style or substance, and the theological problem of evil runs through Milosz's oeuvre in various guises. In other words, he does not stray far from his literary comfort zone in this chapter. By contrast, the descriptions of space travel, new technologies, and biological adaptation in the chapter entitled "An Astronaut's Tale" represent much less familiar territory for the Polish poet. His handling of the new material is occasionally awkward, especially in the account of Lino Martinez's mission to the planet Sardion, which Milosz probably intended to develop further. Nevertheless, the chapter also includes some illuminating transpositions of certain abiding Miloszean themes, as he utilizes the conventions of a foreign genre to open fresh perspectives on old preoccupations.

In particular, the "time travel" made possible by relativity and a ship that can reach 99.5 percent of the speed of light allows Lino Martinez to attain a perspective that Milosz's poetry frequently captures: an isolated subject observing the ravages of time on fragile human bodies from an objective distance, seemingly beyond temporality. This poetic "I" actively seeks to separate itself from the world of the vulnerable flesh, overcoming its own delimited and ephemeral nature by transforming itself into a "pure seeing" that would soar above the world and describe it. Through the character of Lino Martinez, Milosz restages this disembodied perspective within the realist conventions of science fiction, bringing experiential immediacy to the imagined scenario.

The effects of time dilation allow Martinez to abstract himself from the natural processes of aging and death. After the mission, he returns to his home planet to find that many more years have passed for his earthbound acquaintances than for himself, a difference augmented by his access to life-prolonging biotechnologies reserved for the astronaut elite. The eternally youthful Martinez feels a mixture of sorrow and contempt as he meets "a gray, shriveled old woman" who had once entranced him as a young, "olive-skinned" lover. The fact that he does not share her undignified fate greatly distresses him. His own "triumph" over mortality seems hollow and morally suspect, leading him to experience a profound crisis. In an earlier chapter, Karel—another privileged member of the state elite—faces a similar dilemma induced by a sense of forced separation from human corporeality: "Senseless material, senseless brutality. How could he begin to coexist with it?

Could he cease to be an unearthly spirit observing it from beyond?"

Karel's path remains uncertain, but Martinez makes a fateful decision. He abandons his position in the Astronauts' Union, losing access to the regular medical procedures that have kept him young and thus reaffirming his solidarity with suffering humanity. This decision to embrace mortality is tantamount to suicide—a recurring motif throughout the novel. Martinez explains: "If the whole human species had the choice either of losing or winning as we have won, then winning wouldn't be worth it." Martinez discovers that the incarnate, impermanent, and delimited nature of human life is precisely what gives it meaning, while aspirations toward a purer and more enduring existence in separation from these material realities can only lead to alienation and even to contempt for the wretched human herd. As Sławomir Sierakowski puts it in his appendix to the Polish edition: "Longevity is inhuman; it is reserved for God."[7]

Once again, these discoveries echo a regular

preoccupation of Milosz's poetry and essays: a counteremphasis on embodied existence against the "pure seeing" of certain poetic visions. In some of his essays of the same period, he argues that the desire to separate oneself from the material world can easily degenerate into indifference and even malevolence toward human life, an attitude he partly finds in himself, but also in the radical Russian intellectuals who prepared the way for the Bolshevik Revolution and even in American left-wing thinkers of the 1960s.[8] Indeed, Martinez's crack unit in the all-powerful Astronauts' Union is probably intended to bear some resemblance to the party elite of the Soviet Union. As Milosz comes to conceive it, the "disembodied" perspective is not just existential but also strongly political. His characters' revelations reflect his own poetic oscillation between what he sees as a quasi-totalitarian desire for purified distance and a poetry rooted in the mortal "rhythms of the body," confirming the poet's physical connection with humanity in all its frailty and impermanence.

The dominant realist conventions of science fiction allow Milosz to express this central theme perhaps more clearly than anywhere else in his oeuvre. Herein lies the value of *The Mountains of Parnassus*. In essence, the five chapters of the work—together with "Ephraim's Liturgy"—present an interconnected set of thought experiments on broader themes from Milosz's writings: the consequences of scientific or technological progress for the human sense of meaning; the democratization and decline of religion and art; the refinement of state techniques for totalitarian control; and the dangers inherent in the fantasy of human existence without death. The unfamiliar genre of science fiction allows Milosz to take these familiar themes in new directions, presenting the future as accomplished fact in a descriptive realist style, and thus bringing prophecy to life in an act of dystopian world creation.

Despite its incompleteness, *The Mountains of Parnassus* remains Milosz's most comprehensive vision of the future. The prognosis is bleak, though the apparent trajectory of the story's planned development suggests that not all is lost. Amid darkness and decline, a glimmer of hope persists in a remote community of believers who have rebuilt their faith on the foundations of shared ritual and forms of rhythmic speech—the very essence and purpose of poetry, as Milosz understood it. In the fragments of a science fiction novel, Milosz expressed his fears for the future, but perhaps also a tenacious belief in the redemptive power of poetic language.

NOTES

1. For the chronology of Milosz's work on the project, I have drawn on discussions with his son, Anthony Milosz, and on the research of Agnieszka Kosińska, presented in her Afterword to the Polish edition of *Góry Parnasu*. See Agnieszka Kosińska, "Prorok nowego świata," afterword to Czesław Miłosz, *Góry Parnasu* (Warsaw: Wydawnictwo Krytyki Politycznej, 2012), 107–27.

2. Jerzy Giedroyc and Czesław Miłosz, *Listy 1964–1972*, ed. Marek Kornat (Warsaw: Czytelnik, 2011), 517–21. All translations are my own unless otherwise specified.

3. Czeslaw Milosz, "Beinecke Library," trans. Czeslaw Milosz and Robert Hass, *New and Collected Poems, 1931–2001* (New York: HarperCollins, 2001), 523.

4. Sławomir Sierakowski, "Przegrać dla ludzi," appendix to Miłosz, *Góry Parnasu*, 132.

5. Milosz, *"Ars poetica?"* trans. Czeslaw Milosz and Lillian Vallee, *New and Collected Poems,* 240.

6. Czeslaw Milosz, "Science Fiction and the Coming of the Antichrist," trans. Richard Lourie, *Emperor of the Earth: Modes of Eccentric Vision* (Berkeley: University of California Press, 1981), 16.

7. Sierakowski, "Przegrać dla ludzi," 140.

8. In *Visions from San Francisco Bay,* he describes this type of intellectual as "a politicized angel" bearing "all the markings of an inquisitor or servant of the Inquisition." See Czeslaw Milosz, *Visions from San Francisco Bay,* trans. Richard Lourie (New York: Farrar Straus Giroux, 1975), p. 196.

A Note on the Translation

Every translator has felt the temptation to improve the occasional phrase in even the most awe-inspiring work. This inclination grows stronger when the work at hand is a fragmentary typescript published after the author's death, and without the benefit of his participation in a full editorial process. Most Polish readers have noted that certain sections of *The Mountains of Parnassus* fall below Milosz's own exacting artistic standards, though there are also beautiful passages, especially in "The Cardinal's Testament," that call to mind his best writing. Other sections are somewhat obscure in meaning, mostly thanks to the fragmentary nature of the work, but sometimes due to minor glitches in the logical flow of ideas.

In all but the most superficial cases, I have resisted the temptation to make stylistic or semantic renovations, since this would have required considerable guesswork as to the author's intentions. Instead, I have attempted to render the work more or less as Milosz sent it to Jerzy Giedroyc in 1972. Accordingly, *The Mountains of Parnassus* is an imperfect re-creation in English of Milosz's imperfect experiment in the original Polish. Where I have tried to smooth out certain minor infelicities — on the basis that Milosz himself sometimes took the opportunity to make changes in the English versions of his poems — I have done so without altering the sense. Of course, I do not discount the possibility that my interventions have introduced wholly new imperfections into the text.

The most challenging part of the work for the translator is "The Mass of the Catechumens," from the appendix entitled "Ephraim's Liturgy." This text ostensibly transcribes the ceremony of a quasi-Christian ritual, apparently associated with the secret congregation in the Parnassus Mountains. The text includes passages from Ecclesiastes, the Gospel of Matthew, and Psalm

139, all translated by Milosz himself. The section from Ecclesiastes seems to have formed one of the starting points for his later more extensive work in biblical translation, as his rendition of 12: 1–8 does not differ in any way from the version he was to publish in 1982.

Rather than translate from Milosz's own translations of scripture, I have used the Revised Standard Version Catholic Edition and the New Revised Standard Version Catholic Edition, both of which are close in spirit to Milosz's stated aims of modernizing the language while maintaining a "high, hieratic and liturgical" tone.[1] The rest of the mass includes a series of ritual dialogues between "Deacon" and "Congregation," and a "Sermon" in "rhythmic speech." Milosz seems to have invented most of this material himself, though it is firmly based on the style of the Catholic Mass, with certain direct borrowings. In these passages, I have sought to reproduce the same "hieratic" though modern diction that Milosz sustains from his biblical translations.

I thank Anthony Milosz for his generous en-

gagement and helpful advice, Clare Cavanagh
for her inspiration and encouragement, Jennifer
Croft for her constructive and elegant sugges-
tions, Tomek Bilczewski for fruitful discussions
of certain passages, and my colleagues in the
Department of Slavonic Studies at the University of Cambridge. Any missteps are my own.

NOTE

1. See Czesław Miłosz, "Przedmowa tłumacza," *Księgi
biblijne* (Kraków: Wydawnictwo Literackie, 2003), 39.

The Mountains
of Parnassus

Introductory Remarks

To the curious reader of the future, I commend these chapters from a science fiction novel that will never be written. Why will it never be written? Because I don't feel like writing it. Why don't I feel like writing it? It's a question that should be taken seriously. The reason is that the result would be (1) artistically dubious and (2) immoral.

Re (1): In the second half of our century, the novel has become a thankless literary genre. It is a fact that language strives to capture reality, and that the means it employs to pursue this aim can become worn, faded, and conventional, hence our constant headlong flight toward new means of expression. And since the novel was first born of the desire to read "true" stories, even the most pleasing stylistic exercises seem incongruous, as they use devices that somehow break away from the world of things and human relations. Therefore the novelists' quest is understandable, but their success is always suspect, as they seem to fall into the very trap they seek to avoid. The contemporary novel—schooled on stream of consciousness or internal monologue, and tortured by structuralist theories—has strayed so far afield that it little resembles what the novel was once understood to be. We might even say that it has begun to contradict its own essence, since the diabolical boredom emanating from such works is hostile to the very vocation of narrative. It seems that everything has gone awry in the discipline.

The only good novels are those in which reality prevails (for surely the word "reality" still means something), when the reader forgets about language and its devices, and so perhaps I should say that it is not really a question of the means but rather of their new function. Science fiction continues to place its faith in an objective reality, because its creators must pour enormous effort into the construction of one future civilization or another from the ground up, so that the genre can still take the form of an old-fashioned novel. Unfortunately, this type of novel is also internally riven by contradictory tendencies. On the one hand, we find the image of "how things will be," and on the other, we encounter the pressure of modern demands, for we are no longer as good-natured as Jules Verne's protagonists. When science fiction wishes to dispense with nineteenth-century habits in characterization, dialogue, etc., it begins to share the fate of the novel more generally, crossing the boundary beyond which literary fiction loses its significance, for instead of boring ourselves with it, we could just as easily choose to read essays, poems, or scientific works. Here we might take the example of Stanislaw Lem, who began with "naïve" short stories about the future, then later achieved an extraordinary balance with *Solaris*, before growing envious of "serious" novelists and destroying this balance.

As for me, I prefer to admit that I am incapable of resolving the conundrum. Everything is fine as long as I merely show "how things will be," but once I begin to sew the threads together,

putting dialogues into people's mouths, then I
feel intensely embarrassed, as if—the horror!—
I were writing a "novel from life," merely shifting the action to the end of the twenty-first century. We have learned too much not to know all
too well how this works. The author draws on
his own experiences, depicts his acquaintances
under altered names, and so on. I became aware
of my disgust for these procedures upon the
introduction of two female characters, Klaudia
and Tesa, who do not appear in the chapters
printed here. After all, are they really paying
me to expose myself and other people in public? Outright indecency. And if I wished to avoid
this unpleasant feeling, I would have to choose
between settling for the simplified outlines of
a novel for young adults and metamorphosing
into a thoroughly post-Kafkan narrator, which
does not appeal to me at all.

In fact, the reader has the right to interpret
these confessions as the grimaces of a fox pronouncing that the grapes were sour because they
were too high up.

Re (2): After sanguine beginnings, when people were still capable of believing that the discovery of a metal lighter than air could guarantee peace and happiness for humanity, science fiction has mainly consisted of gloomy prophecies. Even H. G. Wells's *The Time Machine* (1895) does not exactly encourage travel into the future. Meanwhile, the events of recent decades have hardly been conducive to expectations of a joyful tomorrow. My chapters will give comfort to nobody, though it's also worth noting that they purport to present the end of the era in which humanity has lost both hope and all sense of historical continuity. In the Parnassus Mountains, a small group of people has formed a kind of community, congregation, or order, and before long they are astonished to discover that similar communities have arisen simultaneously in many other places. Yet the ruling Union still has absolute power. So what will happen next? Of course, literature always fares awkwardly when it strives to depict good people and good intentions, while it portrays evil, cruelty, and failure with accuracy, expertise, and gusto. For this reason, my own novel would be overwhelmingly dark—though there is also another reason. In order to show where hope still lies, I would be forced to write a virtual historiosophical treatise, a task I am prevented from performing by my distaste for long-winded and indeterminate forms.

The purpose of writing is not to terrify and depress people. We have grown weary of the frenzies of "artists" who over long decades have justified the superiority of Art, or the Word, over so-called life, and if we still talk a great deal about the intrinsic (enlightening?) virtues of artistic flights of fancy, then it is largely for fear of ideological servitude. Yet panic is poor counsel. In writing, we cannot help but wonder whether our work will help people or harm them. The truth can never harm. That is certain. Yet the truth always remains complex and multifaceted, and a wholly dark truth probably helps only at times when terrifying or depressing people might induce them to lead a fuller life.

It strikes me that I am incapable of performing this task.

Is it shameful to present mere fragments, while confessing that I will never muster the whole? Perhaps it isn't. Who knows whether I might not even have stumbled upon an experimental genre in spite of myself? For here the reader's imagination will receive no shortage of small stimuli, but also an expansive area in which it can freely glide—which perhaps is better than having everything spelled out and constrained by the twists and turns of the characters' stories. For what hidden threads really link the Arsonists' Association or the HBN with the Union? What kinds of people of both sexes have belonged to the Parnassus community apart from Karel, Ephraim, and Otim (that is, Martinez)? What tactics did the Union adopt when news first reached it (of course, the news had to reach it) of the spontaneous creation of such communities, just as on the planet Arguria? And, since not many people still knew how to use the microfilmed libraries, what did the few with access to old printed books make of the long dead era of the Second Romanticism? And so on and so forth.

Finally, let us hope that the reader will deign to appreciate a certain triumph of the author worthy of imitation—namely, that instead of adding yet another novel to the surfeit of them assailing the shelves of the bookstores, he has managed to restrain himself in time.

Describing Parnassus

The Parnassus Mountains—so named by nineteenth-century travelers, people of a rather poetic disposition—are not especially high, and only three of their peaks are snowcapped in summer: three white pyramids rising at a distance of a few dozen miles from one another over the bluish verdure of the coniferous forest that imbues the tangle of hills, chasms, and valleys with the appearance of a plain. Perhaps Parnassus should have been the name of the highest mountain, the home not so much of the Muses as of the hordes of skiers who descended upon it all year round. Yet by the power of the geographers' decree, it takes the name Tomak, while its two slightly lower companions bear witness to the languages of bygone tribes with the names Onwego and Kitwanga.

On account of their inaccessibility, the forests of the entire mountain range escaped the plunder of the logging industry, and the whole area, spreading over many thousands of square miles, was preserved as a sizable province divided into three administrative units named after three rivers: the Sukunka, the Hominka, and the Barkena. Later, when the Botanists' Union— reinforced by the enormous sums of money invested in it—went to war with the Astronauts' Union, one of the phases of its short-lived preeminence found expression in the merging of the three units to form Parnassus National Park. Much like the other parks created at the time, it contributed to the outbreak of a guerrilla war within the Botanists' Union between the opposing factions of the Naturalists and the Strategists. Since the Naturalists openly proclaimed that the excessive multiplication of the human race was a stain on the face of the Earth, they were in favor of the total closure of the parks, which in their view could form the only defense against the pressure of the vast numbers swarming across the lowlands like ants. The Strategists, on the other hand, taking into account the exigencies of politics and money, believed that it would be possible to limit the damage caused by the three to five million tourists who visited each year. The lovers of so-called nature appeared almost exclusively in the short summer months, if one didn't count the skiers on Mount Tomak. Rain and snow on the ridges scared them off in spring and fall. Otherwise, they kept to the sparse roads and to the campsites densely packed along them. The few marked trails bypassed the areas most abundant in fauna. Stern prohibitions against wandering off these trails were accompanied by warnings of danger. On entering the park, each visitor received a brochure filled with accounts of the misadventures of the careless, who had lost their way and died of hunger or of wounds inflicted by bears. The Naturalists' greatest triumph was the absence of trails along the lakes, on which it was also forbidden to use anything but a rowboat. The curious, wishing to discover what lay at the far end of the longest lake, Nukko, could take an old-fashioned pleasure cruise. Over several hours, they would admire the steep rocky slopes scattered with rings of pine trees resembling the drawings of the Chinese masters, along with waterfalls and Alpine meadows, before the boat sailed into a perennially calm bay protected from the wind, and drew up to the wooden pier. There was not much to see on the shore. A path led to a pavilion filled with charts and photographs of rare tree species, and farther on to a forester's house, where a fenced clearing held a few grazing horses, the only means of locomotion in those untamed parts. The place was not noticeably disrupted by the visitors, as beavers had even built their lodge under the planks of the pier. The Naturalists gnashed their teeth when they saw the main road into the park as clogged in July and August as the artery of a major city, as well as thousands of campfires. And they gnashed their teeth when they saw a tourist dragging a set of moose antlers behind him, clear evidence that he must have ventured into the inaccessible thicket, for a moose would surely not have shed its antlers on the open road. They would find consolation after half an hour's march along a forest path, as the almost total wilderness reassured them of the lack of entrepreneurial spirit among the vacationers.

The River Hominka has its beginnings in a glacier on Mount Onwego. Traveling from the source to its mouth must once have been no small journey, before concrete roads shortened it to a single day. To be precise, the expedition departs not from the source itself, but from the dam that widens the stream into Lake Molelo. A bleak basin at seven thousand feet is fringed by a sickly forest of half-withered firs overgrown with beards of moss. A narrow road, one of the least frequented in the park, drops sharply in hairpin turns along the river, which in turn flows through a winding canyon with such steep walls that the roots of the trees can scarcely cling onto them. The roar of the water echoes off the walls as it foams over the rocks. The canyon gradually becomes less steep, and the river less wild, running here and there into a pool of transparent water over a graceful cascade. In this part of the park, at five thousand feet, there has long been a modest settlement, so that every few miles one stumbles across an inn frequented by the fishermen who come here for the trout. A post office, an inn, and a shop selling everything an angler might need figure on maps as the little town of Onwego.

A little farther down, the forest is increasingly mixed, before finally becoming a broadleaf forest. After another few dozen miles, at around the park's edge, a panorama of grassy hills dotted with scattered buildings unfolds before us, descending in layers down into the valley. A bluish haze suffused with flashes and vague outlines allows us to guess at the structures of the city down below. The road darts away from the river, passing into spiral intersections and over arterial bridges as it descends, until, almost imperceptibly, as we emerge from a kind of half-tunnel, we find ourselves over roofs in the company of shimmering glass skyscrapers. This is a bothersome and tedious section to travel, despite the green strips, lawns, and gardens. But eventually it comes to an end, and—having coasted over

the eight-lane strip of concrete on raised pillars
that cuts across these neighborhoods from north
to south—the traveler once again finds himself
in the park, in a land of meadows, hollows, and
conical rocks capped with trees. And here the
river returns: the same, but different, swollen
with water, uncoiling before the traveler's eyes
in long, gentle curves, with the jetties and houses
of old farms clinging to its banks. Cows—real
cows—stare at it, or at nothing, as they chew
their cud. Near its outlet into the ocean, the Hominka is enormous, and it is difficult to believe
that one has seen it not so long before as a little
stream. Its majestic expanse, where a fishing cut-
ter sailing along under the forested slopes of the
far bank is little more than a white smudge, makes
one think with tenderness of the once famous
names of the much humbler European rivers. In
the Hominka, they fish for sturgeon larger than
men. The fish were almost wiped out last century, which was no surprise considering the scale
of the industry that had established itself at the
mouth of the bay. Here the ocean receives the

waters of two rivers, the second being the Sukunka, which flows from distant regions, swing-
ing northward in an arc from Mount Tomak. It
was the Sukunka, as the old photographs show,
that had once filled the bay with a tangled raft of
floating wood, and—indirectly—the air with the
foul-smelling smoke of the paper mills. Yet the
wood had vanished from the surface of the bay,
and the old factories had vanished, giving way
to gigantic test tubes and furnaces with a very
different purpose.

There was once somebody who found himself on the banks of the River Hominka because his friend Karel had suddenly recalled
that he owned a house in Onwego. In fact, it
was not really a house but simply whatever still
remained of a hundred-year-old ruin that had
long been boarded up and abandoned. Even the
road, which climbed up the hill almost verti-
cally, was overgrown, so they continued on foot,
stopping now and then to catch their breath.
The house stood on the edge of an expansive
plateau, hidden behind a screen of young cedar

trees. A scholar with a famous name in biochemistry had supposedly built it. This was all Karel knew, as he had long since forgotten the name. The rotting planks of the terrace sagged under their steps, so they trod cautiously, especially where one side of the wooden balcony hung suspended over an abyss. Down below, an emerald green river with white rapids glittered under the crests of the overhanging trees. In those moments, as he gazed at the river or raised his eyes to the mountain range, to the single snowy peak that etched its soothing outline into the bluest of skies, somebody said "hmm," and perhaps the entire project was contained in that "hmm." For let us consider what occupied their thoughts: namely, an Earth without fatherhood. Long ago, fathers had existed, towering over the generations like the cool, calm peak of Onwego over the resinous monotony of the forests. People could depend on their wisdom and knowledge, and even rebelling against them gave some sense of security. Yet the fathers had departed, and the children were left alone in their kindergarten.

They—those who exercised power—did not deserve the name of fathers; people referred to them with a mixture of fear and contempt, as they did to the computers playing out semantic tournaments with themselves. Except that the yearning for patriarchal majesty had not disappeared, and many hoped or even believed that their own solitary thoughts corresponded with the heartfelt needs of many solitary others. If the fathers had departed, then the children could surely do nothing else but strive to become their own fathers.

Karel's Adventures

Poor, poor youth. To be born aboard a ship on its way to an unknown destination from an unknown origin, and to grow up learning that there is no port and never will be. The Earth sailed or spun or drifted, or however else we might describe it—just like those artificial earths trapped in their orbits—while its passengers busied themselves with what language picturesquely, though recklessly, described as "killing time," not foreseeing (if language could foresee) how ominous a meaning this expression would assume. Time both terrified and offended us, and thus it had to be destroyed and replaced with intensity of experience in every living moment, so that a great deal could happen before the hands of the clock revealed the passing even of a single minute. If the inhabitants of the terrestrial state communicated with one another at all, it was only to ask the question—"What are you feeling?" Yet because it was impossible to describe these feelings in words, they mostly kept silent.

Like everyone else around him, if Karel was
certain of anything, it was only of the illusory
nature of all phenomena outside the shifting ten-
sions of his own psyche. The gods—whose inde-
structible power had once guaranteed the existence of a legislated world—had disappeared;
the sages—whose august dignity had once made
it possible to imagine that time always moved
toward something, just as it moved in their
orchards from blossom to harvest—had found
no successors. For the painted old men visiting
the clinics for repairs now and then, with their
wrinkles and edemas reminding them that the
motion of the clock hands was insurmountable,
preferred to vaunt their own immaturity—that
is, their withered promise. It is a curious fact
that almost every Earthling was tormented by
the sense that time had lost its venomous monotony for other people: others continued to
feel, and through feeling liberated themselves
from the power of the minutes and hours, while
he alone felt nothing; others were included in a
great something, while he alone was excluded.

In order to join them and experience the short-lived eternity that propelled the line of time, like music in the flourishes of its architecture, he could turn to the M37 current and erotic games. Unfortunately, a person cannot endlessly take pleasure in the current or endlessly amuse himself putting his thing in the other thing. Besides, a considerable if not overwhelming proportion of humanity consisted of the elderly or people unable to curb their genetic deviations from the mental norm. When in bygone days the poet Baudelaire (who was still known to specialists) had said that fornication was the lyric poetry of the people, he had displayed his contemptuous sympathy with the lower classes, who, deprived of access to the higher occupations of the soul, received consolation in their bodies, though this was only fair. But now everybody—even those who long ago might have spent their lives in monasteries or hermitages, in spiritual celibacy, in forced or voluntary asceticism—regarded the renunciation of sex as demeaning, and so they often exposed themselves to failure in the attempt to live up to their image of themselves as normal beings, leading to a substantial increase in the number of suicides.

Karel was eighteen years old when he decided to kill time by killing himself. His loneliness and his sense that life was flowing by while he took no part in it had reached such an extraordinary level of tension that he was forced to conclude that he was gradually disintegrating, and that he would have to put an end to his slide into disorder. He made one failed attempt to heal himself with the help of a female friend, whose Chinese beauty had such an effect on him that—as his ancestors would have put it—he fell in love. He later experienced what the newspapers of the bygone era would have described as a broken heart. Of course, he could have resorted to psychotherapy, but he lacked the will to put himself through it. He also lacked the will to join the Arsonists' Association, which might have been a refuge for him, albeit a temporary one.

Of the various groups and sects promoting

their diverse programs, the Association appealed to him most, for he found in it his own kind of hatred. He was not in the least bit grateful to the generations of so-called intellectuals, who had dismantled their own philosophical toys with light-fingered curiosity. Liberated from phantoms, since all commandments and prohibitions were mirages that rose and fell in the constant communion of people with people, he could no longer ascribe any weight to his morally tormenting dreams, yet it infuriated him to think of these dreams as temporary bubbles of his subconscious, and that he himself was a bubble, whose birth and disappearance would be noted only by statistics. Against this world of forms as fluid as smoke, a world reduced to incest within the human species, the Association offered action without justification or aim. The magnificent fireworks that gushed out of the libraries and laboratories amid the deafening sound of explosions announced a liberation from the slavery into which the mind had driven itself through its very concern with its own freedom.

And the dangers of conspiracy—the diligent
preparation of the climactic moment of fire, the
donning of masks, and running away—all inten-
sified time much more effectively even than the
hand-clapping worshipers of Baal could have
managed. Of course, it was still true that anyone who spent his days moving to the rhythm
of the dance, endlessly chanting the same thing
over and over, could also drive away barren and
fatal thought, coming to inhabit a pure now by
taking part in the nameless. In essence, it all
came down to active or passive means to em-
bark on similar expeditions away from the line
measured by the clock of time. Yet Karel had
become so mixed up that the immediate liquidation of a world stripped of all its flavors and
colors seemed the simplest way.

To exterminate himself, he selected an old-
fashioned method, perhaps because all the
towers and soaring bridges were equipped with
nets or protective glass. Thus human society,
having already unleashed the desire for death
from within itself, attempted with its usual irra-

tionality to prevent at least one form of suicide.
Yet a mere museum piece — a revolver once used
by the police forces of various countries — could
just as easily do the job. Of course, Karel would
not have been such a milksop if he had truly believed in the final end of his personality. But
he was no different from many of his contemporaries, who killed themselves to spite somebody or something in the vague hope that they
would then be able to look on maliciously as
the mother existence who had spurned them received her comeuppance — Karel, too, observed
the rules of theatricality. He had a particularly
strong tendency toward sly calculation, and he
clearly yearned for the gesture more than its result, since he loaded only four bullets. He spun
the cylinder, leaving his extermination uncertain, with the chances a mere four to two — in
short, he played at Russian roulette. He placed
the barrel to his temple and fired, only to hear
the trigger's empty "click."

Things could have turned out differently, and
then he would never have learned the futility of

his gesture. For shortly after this event, which remained known only to himself, there occurred certain developments of immediate concern to both him and everybody else. The new circumstance consisted in the appearance of the HBN, whose existence soon became very real and tangible to all. Nobody was sure whether the HBN, the Higher Brethren of Nirvana, was a legal or illegal institution. Its composition, its connections, and the rationale for its decisions remained secret, though—because, wherever people exist, what is hidden sooner or later comes to light— the most credence was given to a rumor that it was simply an ingenious computer, dependent on its own reasoning alone, but controlled by a secret cell of the Astronauts' Union. As for the aims of its operations, the HBN laid them out openly in leaflets stamped with its initials, which seemed to appear from nowhere. Since excessive multiplication exposed every biological species to the dangers of degeneration and extinction, but one could only condemn the mutual murder of human beings in the paroxysms of passion and cruelty known as wars, the HBN proposed to come to the rescue in a strictly scientific, humanitarian, and detached manner, serving both the species and individual beings struggling under the burdens of life. The HBN announced that it would employ a method known to hunters for centuries as a cull. Before long, it became clear that the HBN was scrupulously delivering on its promise. In fact, its operations did not take the form of thunderbolts striking a timid herd of deer, leaving bloody carcasses in the wake of its flight. Instead, they always involved a simple disappearance, so sudden and complete that a person walking in front of us on the stairs just a second earlier could seem a mere delusion, while a hand clutching a glass appeared to hang suspended in a void. The bundle of molecules held together in the form of a human being lost its unitary quality in a single moment, without any transition through intermediate stages of dissipation, fading, or haziness. It was impossible to establish any rules as to the location or selection of targets. It could happen at home, in the

car, or on the street; neither age, gender, profes-
sion, nor skin color offered any protection — nor
did any particular thoughts or states of soul. The
promise of the rescue was vague enough that its
sentence could strike down both the despairing
and the cheerful. If these were hunts, then the
electronic dogs must have been tracking certain types of genes, though nobody could guess
which ones.

There was clearly a connection between the
suicidal tendencies of the many people like Karel
and the appearance of the HBN. The constant
threat took the sense out of preparing for self-
liquidation, while the present moment regained
something of the flavor it must have held for the
cave people, as they trembled before a night
filled with the roaring of tigers. The secondary
aim of the HBN may well have been to exert a
tonic effect on the inhabitants of Earth, who thus
remained capable, under the right conditions, if
not of rejoicing in the fact that they were alive,
then at least of wanting to live. Indeed, the number of suicides dropped significantly. Comparing

the earlier graph of suicides with the graph of disappearances, it became clear that the latter slightly exceeded the former, suggesting that the overall plan — inaccessible to the masses of mere mortals — must have involved factors beyond the simple depletion of the population.

As was so rightly observed long ago, the adaptive capabilities of our tribe are almost limitless. When one of our ancestors headed into the forest with a club and spear, never to return, the loss simply had to be accepted. And did the families of fighter pilots shot down in battle not have to reconcile themselves to the very same implacable fact? The HBN was met at first with terror. Yet many of the noble impulses of universal compassion had reached a crisis point during the War of the Lovers of Racial Peace, when fears over the poisoning of the planet had brought people in their millions to attack one another with knives, so that one could say without exaggeration that all had swallowed a substantial dose of callousness and indifference. In any case, it now appeared that man had always felt more indifference toward the deaths of others and more resignation toward his own death than had ever been captured by a language that dramatized the experience from the simple need for expression. The holes caused by the HBN soon healed over, and life continued along the same old track, even if the nonappearance of a lover at a café sometimes meant that she no longer existed, and a mother could enter her baby's room to find an empty crib.

The experiences of that night, when Karel had played his game of roulette, turned out to carry certain prophylactic advantages, as they immunized him against the HBN. Something had snapped in his head, so the night must have constituted more than a mere performance for his own delectation. He had landed in a zone of clarity, inner composure, and perfect functionality, while his handwriting formed an external sign of the transformation. Instead of his earlier clumsy scrawl, which had seemed uncertain whether to slant to the left or right, he began—almost from one day to the next—to set down compact letters, clear and confident of their direction. He also noticed a sudden expansion of his mental abilities, as if a veil had been torn away to reveal something he sensed was there, but did not recognize. He decided that from then on he would make full use of these abilities. By devoting themselves to learning in the schools known as universities, people had once merely fulfilled the regulations justifying the existence of these institutions, which now belonged to the past. From the moment they had been appointed another task—namely, to enrich the concept of play, and with it to occupy all those children from the age of seventeen to twenty-five for whom there was no employment—learning had been regarded as a caprice or dubious privilege of the few. They were known as "the hardheads," and there were enough of them to sustain the economy. Karel's successes were so substantial and rapid that he seemed destined to take his place among the chosen ones abducted by the Astronauts' Union. In the end, he managed to avert this fate, as he had no desire to become a mere counting mule, a genius thanks to the chemical substances that the highest authorities dispensed only to their own.

Both during his studies and in his later career, when everything he did was a success, he discovered a disquieting gift in himself. While others called it his good fortune or his intelligence, he himself almost felt fear, as if he had received too much. We constantly find ourselves within an ever-changing system of elements in unceasing motion, and our defeats usually spring from ignorance of the rules according to which this motion unfolds. Karel had convinced himself that he could predict how the elements would behave, and into what new combinations they would arrange themselves. In the game with fate, he could see his opponent's cards, as if they were transparent. A suspicion began to grow inside him, soon becoming a conviction, that his diligence and mechanical sense of duty had made him a dangerous psychopath, all the more so since his psychosis was hidden, unlike that of the more obvious lunatics running about with flowers in their hair. In other words, his gift was a payment, and by using it he had been forced to make a deal. But a deal with whom? There is no need to enter into his reasons; perhaps he wanted to suffer—anything to satisfy his desire for justice or decency. Let it suffice to say that he experienced recurring cycles of pain, not in his body, but still acute. It usually began as a gradual worsening of the state in which he permanently existed, accustomed to it as if to a nagging toothache. Certain signs warned him that an attack was approaching, and he was even able to calculate how many days it would take to arrive. It took the form of an inner trembling that rose to fever pitch, as if some unknown force were raging inside him, pulverizing him from within, lasting from two to three weeks on each occasion. If not for a supreme effort of will, he would have been incapable of anything but lying down and trying to find a position to appease his adversary—for instance, it helped to curl up into a ball and assume the fetal position. Yet Karel learned to impose on himself the normal conduct of his work, never giving himself away to those around him, which was such a difficult task that he admired himself for accomplishing it. The ever longer chain of these imperious acts of self-control produced an ever stronger discipline within him, and he thought of it as his secret, as his Samson's mane.

So this was Karel's lot, even as he raked in the honors and money. Supposedly worthy of envy, but personally convinced that they should be treating him in a sanatorium, which would still have been an unbearable humiliation: to be struck down by the HBN as a patient whom scientific inventions would send off into a state of artificial bliss. No, better for what was to fall upon him to fall, in the midst of ridiculous and freely accepted activities, and even in freely accepted illness. At least Karel's periodic affliction and the constant nagging background were congenial to thought, or perhaps even sprang from thought, and he had no intention of renouncing thought, even if he knew that there could be no remedy for him as long as thought still turned inside his head. Perhaps in the end it was not even a question of thought, but rather of a way of seeing. If he were to have stripped a woman naked on the street with his eyes, it would simply have been consoling, as the pink nipples and the dark triangle under her dress would have quickened the beating of his heart with animal warmth. Yet he stripped both women and men with his eyes; he stripped them of their clothes, but also of their bodies and of time itself, constantly plagued by the insufficient reason for their existence, and for his own. In costumes, finery, and trinkets, in total submission to the collective crazes and fashions of the crowd, so that not a single particle belonged to them, he saw the repulsive ridiculousness of nothingness dressing up as nothing. Meanwhile, the city exuded a particular aura or vibration, which he perceived with a sixth sense. From the spires of its buildings, from the aerial roads, from the docks and airports, from its pulsating glow, the city slammed into him as a cross between the buzzing of an enraged bee and the hiss of a venomous snake poised to strike. Senseless material, senseless brutality. How could he begin to coexist with it? Could he cease to be an unearthly spirit observing it from beyond? So-called adjustment was not Karel's strong suit; in fact, it was doubtful that anyone could have managed it.

On Methods of Governing

Karel heard that Ephraim had returned from seven years in exile, and he met him shortly afterward. He found before him a strong, stocky man with a black beard heavily streaked with gray, and the beady eyes of a cunning animal. In the very idea of exile there was something of the relict from the distant past, and this interested him. Long ago, the more energetic rulers had made the strange assumption that the minds of the ruled were a threat if they could not be convinced by persuasion or fear. Enormous sums were spent on shaping and convincing those minds by means of so-called culture — or, as it was also known, literature and art. A certain predetermined percentage of the population was locked up in prisons, in barracks ringed by barbed wire, or exiled into the wilderness, not necessarily because these prisoners themselves represented the seeds of rebellion, since this was impossible to ascertain, but rather because the very fear of ending up behind bars had a salutary effect on the others. These primitive methods reflected the primitive level of technology. The simplest things are generally the most difficult to discover, and, in this case, it soon became apparent that the state of mind of citizens was more or less irrelevant to the exercising of power, and that—with the exception of those belonging to the Astronauts' Union—it was best to leave them to their own devices within certain sensible limits. Of course, the freedom of the various clubs, groups, and teams was ever only ostensible; some suspected even the Arsonists' Association of secret dependence on the Union, which could have been truth or fiction. Above all, the great transformation should be attributed to the disappearance of the so-called investigations, which soon became unnecessary. Only the form remained of the old penal codes linking the punishment to the crime, though this form would stubbornly persist for some time, pedantically molding imaginary crimes when something else was really at stake—namely, improper tendencies of mind. Eventually, a turning point would arrive with the publication of

The Theory of Individuality, which soon became a foundational work, while the Astronauts lauded its author, Professor Motohiro Nakao, as one of their great organizers.

Ephraim had been exiled to Seal Island—an unusual sentence, though it did not contradict the premises of *The Theory of Individuality*. Professor Nakao's achievement had been to break down individuality into its fundamental components, which he then submitted to various arithmetic operations. In his well-known example of two children placed in identical conditions, Nakao demonstrated that a single minor divergence in the reception of sense impressions could initiate two different "tracks," and that one needed only a certain amount of data to understand the direction of these "tracks," just as opinion polls were not conducted among ten or twenty million individuals, since it sufficed to take a sample of typical attitudes, which would then check out mathematically. Considering the diversity of individuals, multiplied by genetic chaos (as if the genes kept playing tricks on the

geneticists), Nakao taught that the focus of attention should be exclusively on those particular "tracks" of perception that might turn out to
be harmful to the rational social order defended
by the Astronauts. The need for tedious police
surveillance of suspects disappeared, as did the
need to lock them up in prison to submit them
to investigations that were unpleasant to both
sides, since the computer (which was very toler-
ant) could make a diagnosis on the basis of easily
accessible and apparently insignificant data.

But why had they not used Cocooning on
Ephraim? No one could guess. Cocooning was
another invention of Professor Nakao; it had led
to the complete disappearance of what were now
considered barbaric practices of the central authorities. The mere states of somebody's mind,
and even the most subversive ideas flowing from
these states, could bring no harm to the planetary order. Only communication among eccen-
trics and the dissemination of their ideas called
for preventive measures. In order to communicate, people had to be tuned in to the same

wavelength, or work mentally at the same speed. By interfering with this ability—for instance, by slowing or accelerating the speed of a person's thoughts to deny him access to other people's thoughts—the potentially dangerous individual suddenly found himself inside an invisible cocoon. The cocooned person would speak, but fail to understand why his logical and convincing arguments sounded like incomprehensible babble to everyone else. This was even more confusing after the era when he could still have dated his problem with language back to a certain visit paid to the Welfare Bureau, perhaps none too willingly, though even then his conversation with a polite official would have borne none of the hallmarks of police harassment. In those days, Cocooning still required a large stationary machine to work on the patient through the wall. The moment the process ceased to depend on a particular location, nobody knew whether he was having trouble finding a common language with others because he had been cocooned or simply because the natural development of his own tendencies was disturbing his interpersonal relations. Of course, there was never any shortage of people who were simply cocooned by nature, so to speak, and for them there was no need for any additional treatment. But others exhibited such a high level of immunity that the Cocooning had no effect on them. Either Ephraim belonged to the second category or the decision had been made for other reasons—in any case, he received the order to leave and move to a region he neither knew nor would ever have chosen to visit of his own free will.

The Cardinal's Testament

What was hidden behind the thick, convex glasses of the little librarian in Miramar? Were those flashes of malice, irony, or good-natured humor? What was he thinking? What did he approve? What was he mocking? He had suggested to Ephraim the tape of an annual compilation of a magazine with a Latin title that had appeared at the end of the era of the Second Romanticism in such a small print run that it was doubtful that any copies of it had survived anywhere. Casually and in passing (since he was busy holding forth on the poor quality of the paper used by similar publishing houses, always yellowing and falling apart after a few years), the librarian mentioned the name of a certain Petro Vallerg. Of course, Ephraim immediately found the issue of this esoteric *revue* that had announced the painful loss of Cardinal Vallerg, colleague and friend, together with the promise that the magazine would soon publish a manuscript entrusted to it by the deceased. The next issue included the cardinal's

composition: a last will, an appeal to the faithful, or perhaps simply a confession.

So I have lived through my life, though when
I was a young boy this seemed impossible. Old
age is upon me now, in the knobbles of a bony
hand like a metal vise, in elbows that grow ever
sharper, in the rows of perpendicular notches
around my mouth, and old age is inside me, in
the mellowing and muting of the sorrowful feeling that this is it, that there will be nothing more
than this. I was the only child of a pious mother,
and I have fulfilled her expectations of me. Now
I still see her as she walks home along the street
from the market carrying a basket of vegetables,
or as she washes the window, sweeping a rag
across the glass against the backdrop of a spring
cloud, since the sequence of time has been dis-
turbed, and there is no division between earlier
and later, just as there is no division between
more important and less important. Frail, fragile, and lonely, always excluded from the games
of my peers, I entered the seminary because this

was her unspoken wish, or perhaps because the fear of incomprehensible, brutal, alluring, and repugnant life tormented me at night. I was not as frail or as fragile as I had imagined, but it took me some time to understand that what paralyzed me and divided me from others was my aristocratic fastidiousness, though there was nothing aristocratic about our family of bus drivers and postmen. Vocation? Who can say what a vocation is? I learned not to delve into the question, however many times I may have used the word.

How difficult it is to live through life for a C minus. And I suppose one gets a C simply for living, so only the minus is my own. I have never kept a diary or written any memoirs, and now is surely not the time to begin. When I was growing up there was a general craze for recording the most graphic details or depicting them on the screen, but my objection to this violation of the human right to one's own self was so strong that I respected only those who never made a sound. Now I endure with all my past, which returns in dreams, and — to my relief — will never be known to anyone. Yet if my past does not simply amount to nothing, then it might offer proof of God's existence to nonbelievers, since someone must know it, after all. Let it suffice for me to confess to hours, months, years, and decades of longing, longing for what was quite ordinary to others, yet was always denied me. Not just the constant torture of the body's impulses, but the imagined happiness of couples when I saw them holding hands, their enchantment with the air, a curve in a wall, a tree, a flower, fragrance and color, a rapture with its source in the amorously awakened body. When I closed my eyes, temptation enticed me with the rustle of fabrics, the intonations of speech, the very rhythm of everyday human life. Even when I had no desire to listen, the flutters and vibrations of omnipresent human space nuzzled against my cheek. I never held it against my colleagues that they left — and more and more of them kept leaving, until in the end only a handful of us persevered in celibacy. I never held it against them, because it is almost beyond human strength for a person to start the day having told himself in advance that nothing will happen to renew him from without or to nourish his sensual needs, and that only thought is permitted.

My contemporaries ceased to be capable of fasting or asceticism, for they drew a dividing line between what was natural and healthy—that is, happiness—and what was unnatural and morbid—that is, unhappiness. And one can never overcome happiness with unhappiness; happiness can be opposed only by more happiness. For me, the demonic insidiousness of sex was not an invention of Christianity, which supposedly had destroyed the splendid indulgence of the pagans by condemning certain physiological functions as dirty. I never supported those fervent theologians who strove to blur or conceal the Christian dread of the diabolical temptations, proclaiming the blessings of hygiene with splendidly modern openness and ever old-fashioned sweetness and light. After all, one need not share the views of the Manichaeans, Bogomils, and Albigensians to agree that nothing so entangles us in the world

of falsity and pain as the very instinct that pro-
longs our existence in this world. Oh, the body
itself is not dirty; if anything about it is dirty, it
is only the death prepared within it. Neither is
animal instinct dirty, except that—unhappily—
it is not instinct alone that works within us, but
also the consciousness inextricably intertwined
with it. If we must be children to enter the Kingdom, then our childishness ends where innocent
trust ends and the greed of possession begins.
What was natural and healthy for the opponents
of asceticism signified to me an acceptance of
their condition as the only sick creatures among
all living things. For it is a fatal disease to have
instinct tainted with consciousness or consciousness tainted with instinct.

In the name of the Kingdom. I made sac-
rifices, not to obtain happiness, but in order
that an otherworldly happiness might be possible, as if it might suffice for at least one man
to reject the world from a boundless desire that
nothing could satisfy. The very prayer for the
coming of the Kingdom can itself be the King-

dom, bringing a fullness—it is hard to explain—
more powerful than any longing for a woman's
playful hand to cover one's eyes. This does not
suggest strength of faith; it is not for me to ex-
toll my own constancy or steadfastness. I have
doubted deeply and often, finding refuge only
in the exercises that Ignatius of Loyola set his
followers, transporting myself by force of will
through space and time, in reverse, past winters receding into falls, springs receding into
winters, funerals almost simultaneous with the
begetting of carcasses imprisoned in black cas-
kets with nickel-plated clasps, the last emper-
ors shrinking into children on their thrones
and then being born as the founders of dynas-
ties, cities shaved of streets and squares until
they became but a single street, the first street,
in reverse, back to a small province of the Roman Empire, to Galilee, when Jesus was teaching there. Guided by the will, my imagination
led me along paths through the fields as an invisible shadow beside his disciples. Did I not remember his words: "But be of good cheer; I have

overcome the world"? On the paths of Galilee, as an unhappy soul with no consolation beyond the far from unwavering conviction that these disciples had faithfully translated his words into Greek, that they had not embellished them with their own fantasies, I said to the Teacher: "Lord, you alone can heal me of my unbelief, but if you are merely a madman, proclaiming that you were there before Abraham, if you did not rise from the dead and Thomas did not touch your palms punctured by nails, then still I wish to accompany you into death and nothingness. Beloved, dearest one, if you—the highest accomplishment that humanity has attained and will ever attain—fell victim to delusion, then there is not and will never be a purpose with which man may endow his life, and therefore, following you, may he curse this universe without beginning and without meaning. For who am I to demand for myself more than you demanded, with nowhere to rest your head?"

The body is shaped not only by the training to which we subject it in the gymnasium or on the sporting field, but also by sacrifice and by the rechanneling of constantly dissipating energy in a single direction. The face I scrutinize in the mirror bears the marks of spiritual battles, and, in spite of my age, I feel in my movements the precision of their responsiveness. Yet this hard-won, vigilant bodily attention has been the cause of another, more difficult battle. A wrestler walks among his flabby, ungainly, and corpulent peers, superior to them by all the hours he has devoted to his training. I was a wrestler with little generosity of spirit, and what constantly assailed me was contempt for others. They scuttled after their petty amusements, chasing money, tipping back their glasses, wolfing down steaks, writhing about in bed, and I was forced to recognize them as brothers and sisters, though my own fortified mind had weakened or annihilated the temptations that seduced them. When a smoker gives up cigarettes, smoke begins to annoy him; a vegetarian turns away in disgust when a ruddy-faced man at a neighboring table ties up his serviette and cuts into a bloody piece of meat; the glut-

tony of lovers is irrational to a person who tells
himself that the charms of breasts and thighs
have no objective existence, while a dog lying
in the bedroom where the couple is locked in
amorous embrace yawns indifferently. The pride
of the body, ornamented, hips swaying, feeding
on admiring glances—but what would happen
to it on a deserted island? No, neither their fashions in clothing, music, or performance nor their
clashes over money brought me any closer to
them, but perhaps only the ambition common
to us all—a defiant, stubborn passion, especially
strong among recluses and old men, sneering
at the humility imposed by reason, and even
at prayer. My ambition wore many disguises.
One of them was contempt, and who could say
that compassion had not been another. Yet only
compassion would save me. They grabbed hold
of one another, huddling together in their unreal spectacle, and yet every one of them was
his own singular failure and his own singular lament. Now I can only cling to the hope that in

my contempt I have accepted their failure and their lament as my own.

I enjoyed my investigations into the history of the Church; I did not enjoy discovering the truth about it. The astonishing success of bumpkins and ignoramuses who defeated all the knowledge and genius of antiquity. Was it their success or the even more astonishing failure of the vanquished? In an era of universal ennui and no ultimate purpose, it seems that the ancients would have prostrated themselves before any who could promise a swift end to the world. But those others—mild and quiet-hearted, believing fervently in the ever unfulfilled prophecy of a second coming, by and by—carried a punitive sword up their sleeve. I dare say that very few before our own times have had so much cause to ponder the disgust the first Christians felt for the open iniquities and boastful crimes, the murders in the arena for public entertainment, and the lewd public rituals. Yet when Saint Augustine invoked Plato in *De Civitate Dei,* it was the Plato

who had desired in the name of moral principles
to impose prohibitions, establish tyranny, and
banish poets from the republic. The very same
Augustine dismissed the gods as devils, thus
populating the wilds and forests of Europe with
them for centuries, where, in exile, they terror-
ized and tempted traveling monks, or received
veneration from the hidden enemies of the new
order at witches' Sabbaths. No, I never allied
myself with the liquidators of our estate, who,
simply because the Church had lost its power,
began to bemoan its earlier severity and intol-
erance. It was all too easy for them to beat their
breasts and drape themselves with the robes of
lovers of harmless benevolence, while secretly
thinking that, if the Church had not used the
stake and the sword of obedient monarchs in
the critical thirteenth century, little would have
remained of Christianity, while Europe would
surely have met the fate of stagnant India, with
its own form of Buddhism—the Cathars. My
position was always clear. I was not ashamed of
the game the Church had played with a certain

personage bearing little resemblance to Jupiter or Venus, Juno or Priapus, or perhaps only insofar as they were all worldly gods, while he bore the name of the Prince of This World. I certainly do not mean to suggest that either overtly or behind the mask of an atheist sympathizer I ever defended the last doomed positions, declaring myself in favor of our now impossible worldly power. Yet today, when the edifice of two millennia has crumbled, we may see the consequences of the shame that induced us to reject the relative good simply because it was only relative.

Naught but dust—dust the sumptuous draperies, gilding, and marbles, and behind them the power and money of kings, princes, owners of the human flock, slave traders, pious tormentors of peasants. Dust the miters and thrones, and baldachins, and sweet figurines of a pink baby Jesus, and Madonnas clad in roses, and collators' pews, and carved altars, and all the countless Sundays, when the sound of military trumpets rang out for the Elevation, and the cannons answered with a salvo from the walls. Ever at the gates of hell, choosing one thing or another from what was permitted: celebrate the holy day, do no harm to widows and orphans, perform penance for murder and adultery. And tithes, and fiefs, and grand buildings, and saving the souls of heretics by breaking their arms and legs on the wheel. Yet I took solace in what the Church had once been, since no purely human institution similarly depraved could have survived. And if history is so opaque and ambiguous that we can never establish the facts of the past, if everything that happened long ago stretches and contracts in the testimony as if in a multitude of distorted mirrors, then at least here we might find the one and only continuity in the vast archive gathered over the centuries, the one and only thread accessible to our understanding. And had it not been for the Church, then where would they have crawled on the stumps of their limbs, where would they have hobbled on their staffs and crutches, where would they have wept tears to release them from silent torment, certain, absolutely certain that every last day and hour would be weighed upon the scale, and that, for the saints on the icons, for the Jesus of wood and plaster, for the crowned Virgin, they were more than merely a kneeling crowd, but rather individual men and women, known by name from the days of their birth? While collaborating—yes, without doubt—in their oppression, the mother Ecclesia guaranteed them there before the altar more than mere equality with the rich and powerful, but the majesty of a call addressed to them, the lowly.

The dust of form. In truth, over my long life, only on a few occasions did I participate in the repeated rite of the Last Supper as I felt it should be repeated. And even the hoarse brass trumpets and baroque opera on the balconies of the choir met only with forbearance in me, since in ritual we always yearn to reach beyond form, and yet this is never possible. A gesture intended to be the purest and most sincere expression of the spirit petrifies into form, retreating into it and surrendering to it. I am guilty of consenting to this, though ultimately nothing but consent was possible; I am guilty of the sermons that I recall now with bitterness, when instead of staying silent after the reading of the Gospel, hiding my face in my hands and awaiting the gift of tongues, I heard the wooden tone of my own words. People are right to parody priestly prayers, chants, aspergillums, processions of portly capons in sweeping women's gowns, for the priest parodies himself like an actor who has performed the same play too many times. And the reform of the liturgy, though it was supposed to extract him from this theater and bring him closer to the congregation of previously passive viewers, only resulted in panic, adding to the general panic that seized Christians when it was announced that the immutable and sacred had always been conventional and historical, and that now they would have to derive a newly conventional sacred from themselves.

So it had to be that a house eaten from within by termites, still covered in external splendor, lost its roof and walls, which collapsed in the attempt to replace a single beam, though it was not immediately apparent in the cloud of dust that the walls had gone. Nobody will ever know what John XXIII was really thinking when he announced his *aggiornamento*, whether he really intended only to adapt the Church to the new demands of the time. But adapt to what, if they who placed their votive candles before the images of saints no longer believed in immortality, not because they did not want to believe— indeed, they wanted very much to believe, even stubbornly pretending to themselves that they did believe—but because their imagination had been incapacitated, and could no longer hold a Heaven, a Purgatory, or a Hell to receive them? Could one hope for adaptation when the will to faith had replaced faith itself, bringing the suspicion of falsity to every choral song and every prayerful joining of hands, while religious art— which, like every form of art, both attempts to lie and is unable to lie—had demonstrated its own impossibility? Perhaps John XXIII had other, hidden intentions, preparing the distant future through the fall of that which was destined to fall. Perhaps he foresaw the new epoch, when a name inflected by the phonetics of barbarian languages—Yesu, Giêsu, Isos—would cease to be a protective incantation or a curse, as it would simply have been forgotten, when it would be impossible to turn to the Virgin goddess with entreaties for a happy marriage, and no patron saint could help a person find his lost keys. Only then, he might have thought to himself, would certain people, a precious few, stumble upon the old track in their homelessness, for it was not for man to flee from God.

I witnessed it all, though—I confess—not without stifled laughter. They were so ashamed of their centuries of hypocrisy, of their alliances with monarchs and the rich, of their babble to the injured and humiliated about the prize awaiting them in the afterlife, that now they swore to turn Christianity into action, incarnating it in social morality and working for the coming of the Kingdom of God on Earth. Oh, original sin is reactionary indeed, weakening any enthusiasm for marches in the vanguard or the ardent defense of noble public causes, and so they even corrected Freud wherever he was too pessimistic in his appraisal of the possibility of the natural man's triumph. Original sin embarrassed them, so they served it up in their catechisms as a kind of biblical legend. Angels and demons embarrassed them, so they happily sent this invisible host off into the land of metaphor. After all, they assured people in their sermons, we have always praised the goodness and beauty of creation, so let us love one another, and the Earth will become a paradise. Unfortunately, much better specialists in the organization of universal happiness already existed, managing perfectly well without the Old and New Testaments, and, before long, they—so ardent and eager—would find themselves in the role of condescendingly tolerated helpers. One cannot deny the strength of character of all those seminarians and young priests who justified their work as activists by appealing to scripture, only to renounce it later for political doctrine when they saw how it departed from the correct way of thinking. At least they

were more consistent than those who remained
torn, while still prepared in their own sermoniz-
ing way to glorify the religion of man, which was
now finally alluring enough to replace the religion of the stern Judge.

The gates of hell were far away . . . They did
not deign to recall what Montesquieu had foretold, and what would soon come to pass: that
Protestantism would disappear, and that what
Protestantism had been, Catholicism would become. They themselves labored over the fulfill-
ment of his prophecy, not by imposing morality,
but by dissolving faith in morality, turning faith
into a concession from the prince. Called into
being by collective desires, this prince was supposed to be good, though certain doubts about
his virtues could not save the concessioners who
worked for him. When an individual is delighted
neither by reasons of State nor by the rhetoric of
social norms, he will find meager consolation in
a choice between lessons in civic morality and
the Church as a troop of boy scouts trained in
an additional politeness useful to the authorities.

For what is he to choose when one way or the other he will be equally homeless? And so was this new Catholicism not also doomed to meet the fate of the Protestant sects?

They wished to redeem themselves and find forgiveness, and nothing inclined them to remorse more than the image of a devil with a pitchfork driving souls down into a fiery cauldron, and so there was no end to their sniggering at this character to ingratiate themselves with progress. Their clientele no longer believed in eternal flames, the apple from the tree of knowledge, or—let us be frank—in the resurrection of the body, so how could they teach them of the dragon, the serpent, or the horned monster lurking in the darkness and waiting for somebody to devour? The traders in the marketplace knew how to sell their merchandise, offering religion in humanitarian packaging and assuring the flock that if Jesus had been crucified, it was because he had been a pacifist, a social worker, and a leader of the oppressed. There was no role here for the *diabolos*—the slanderer, the informer, the

falsifier—and it could not have been he who had
tempted Jesus in the desert, as he was merely a
figure of speech.

They amazed me, because right next door,
right behind the building in which the rhythmical clapping of hands reinforced their smiling
and progressive good sense, the possessed—
those whom the Bible calls *daimonizomenoi*—were
babbling and thrashing about in convulsions.
In fact, never before had their number been so
great, even taking general population growth
into account; and never before had their voices,
electronically amplified, carried so far, reaching
the ears of all. Practical proof of the energy of
the Evil One was plain to see, but they, fearful
Christians, would regard the acceptance of this
proof as an embarrassment to their modernity.
Yet somebody's malevolent presence was un-
mistakably imposing itself, for it was difficult to
imagine that such perverse powers could have
emerged from the people themselves, or that
Christians were now the mainstays of a sheeplike
cheerfulness of spirit, nibbling the green grass in

the valley of the best of all possible worlds. Their contemporaries without faith in God were more inclined to believe in a malicious and omnipotent demiurge, the signs of whose prowess the Earth had supplied in abundance. There were even those who prayed to him, hoping to gain his favor, celebrating black masses openly or under some other name.

I did my duty as much as I could, and perhaps it will be recorded in my favor that I wished to contribute as little as possible to the turmoil in their minds. Yet I knew that it was not for me or a few other like-minded souls to reverse a course of events ordained since before the beginning of time. The apostles had not been mistaken when they carried around the shores of the Mediterranean Sea the news that the hour was late; they had only been mistaken when they reckoned that hour in the years of a human life, for the late hour of history is indifferent to our measure of centuries and millennia. "Nevertheless, when the son of man cometh, shall he find faith on the earth?" Luke conveyed the son of

man's question, but did he understand it? Everything has unfolded as it was meant to unfold,
and every tree is known by its fruits. I have not
looked for signs in the Church of domesticated
humanitarianism and hygienic obsequiousness,
and neither will they who come after me look for
signs in a Church that will doubtless lose even
the memory of the Last Supper, replacing *agape*
with the warmth of animal passions. Once again,
He—the judge of the living and the dead—will
choose whomsoever He wishes, confounding all
human calculations: not from among those who
carry the symbol of reconciliation with Him, but
from among apostates and pagans, and they will
not be able to comprehend whence and why an
unknown force seizes them against their will,
and whither it carries them.

Now I am weary, and I reflect with relief that
I shall not have to look at the misfortunes fashioned by people with their own hands, or rather
with their own minds, or resist the temptation
to brush it all off with a shrug, saying simply
that they get what they deserve. I can dare only

to hope that my contempt has been directed against them as a collective (after all, surely the collective, so completely, so radically different from Man, deserves contempt), and not against them as individual beings. The Church was not merely a collective—for this always stands at the gates of hell—but also a community of beings transformed in that which was unique in each of them. I shall not have to look. I am a desiccated insect that has frozen on a leaf, and now warms itself in the last rays of the sun before the coming of winter. When I am gone, the long winter will have its share of sunny days, its joy, and levity, and laughter, though always accompanied by a piercing chill. It is not so bad to have nothing, as I have nothing—neither this bodily shell, which will soon be taken away, nor the glory of immortal works, nor the treasures stored up for a brief time in fading memory—nothing but the Promise.

An Astronaut's Tale

My real name is Lino Martinez. As I've already mentioned, I was a member of the Union for a long time, and I took part in the expedition to Sardion. But just in case, and irrespective of what might still happen, I want to tell the story of how things were with me, and why I'm here. It won't be easy, so I'll try to start from the beginning.

I don't come from the kind of family where you get to go to a Union school as a child, benefiting from the privileges of your parents. I was selected and trained up because my tests were exceptionally good, but it all started rather late. As a child, I was raised by my mother; I never knew my father. At school, I didn't get along too badly, since I had a strong physique, a love for games, and even some talent for learning. Still, I didn't escape without the odd complication. At the time, there were still plenty of Christians in my native region of the Andes, and my mother belonged to a church. I say "at the time," and I should explain that my age is quite dif-

ferent from what you might imagine from my
appearance. My mother attached great significance to Christian practices; she forced me into
them, with some success, so that for a certain
time I believed sincerely—or so it seems to me
now—and prayed every day. But the crisis soon
came, and it was painful, probably triggered by
my aversion for our priest when I discovered that
his robes were only a disguise, that he was pretending not to be what he really was. In truth,
he was an officer of the Welfare Bureau, over-
seeing the faithful on the orders of his superi-
ors. The crisis would have come sooner or later,
but it's worth mentioning this detail. Apart from
this, I exhibited a morbid timidity entirely unex-
pected in such a healthy and cheerful young boy,
less toward my contemporaries than toward my
elders, so that when my mother sent me to the
shops I would fight battles with myself, my heart
beating violently until I almost fainted, blushing
and blanching, before I could even muster up
the courage to cross the threshold of the store.
This timidity gradually subsided, but it disap-

peared for good only when the Astronauts took
me away to their unit, though I wouldn't swear
that it wasn't precisely for this reason that they
took me in the first place, since this symptom,
with the right other factors, can be a variant—
in other words, such people can acquire excep-
tional courage through therapy.

I was a mature adolescent, almost a young
man, when my mother died in an accident, and
then I lived for a while with distant relatives.
This was to be a very important period for me,
but I'll return to it shortly. For now, I want to
talk about the training I received from the Astronauts, though only in very general terms. It's
not that I'm worried about breaking the prohibition—I couldn't care less—but I was trained
in such a way that the prohibition is still buried
deeper than my will. In short, I would describe it
as follows: war offered the highest test of human
energy drawn into oneness, into a single node,
and so our training was modeled on military
discipline, instilling all the soldierly virtues in us.
It goes without saying that this didn't mean the

methods of armies, with their tin soldier drills, uniforms, and blind obedience. We were the conscious and faithful soldiers of humanity, and the emphasis was always on consciousness and faith in the goal. But also on self-consciousness. There were plenty of solitary sessions in front of screens to check how our brains were behaving. We were supposed to attain the greatest possible harmony between being and thinking. Naturally, it was impossible to achieve total calm— the even, barely wavering line of Alpha current, as when we put a cat in front of the oscillograph. But the violent peaks and troughs of Beta current as it recorded restless thought could be subdued with practice, so that the bright line began to undulate slowly and evenly, the Beta acquiring something of the equilibrium and softness of Alpha current.

They demanded much of us, and the number of hours we worked was unimaginable for anyone outside the Union. I said I had a talent for learning, but the standards of those on the outside were irrelevant to us, since our brains could master such an enormous body of material only thanks to daily doses of substances whose chemical composition I myself do not know. Under the influence of those substances, a kind of splitting occurred: one part of us remained astounded by the rapid operations of our own minds, and the fact that we were able to remember so much. All this strenuous work, including the work on ourselves, took us farther and farther away from ordinary people every day. Alcohol was banned, and we were forbidden under pain of the harshest penalties from trying the M37 current. Strict sexual asceticism was also enforced as long as we were in the unit.

I fully identified myself with the Union: I was the Union, and the Union was me. I studied its history in detail, and I regarded the boundary drawn between us and the rest of humanity as right and just in the light of its achievements. I also regarded our privileges as right and just, if only because we had paid for them with a commitment that others had renounced. Besides, one of the privileges was ours simply because it could not be extended to others. Of course, I speak of a certain right that would have led to general catastrophe if it had not been reserved for us alone: the right to the prolongation of life. They couldn't even handle the short lives they had been given, often resorting to suicide, so what would they have done with hundreds of years, not to mention the problem of the over-population of the planet? We, on the other hand, were ready to sacrifice ourselves if necessary, conscious that we would be sacrificing more than they, with their short-lived bodies.

I cannot describe how much I changed as a result of our training, which lasted a very long time—for years. Each of us was both passive and swift in the pursuit of our common aim, like an arrow in flight. We were the representatives of the species on earth and in the galaxy, and we had been imbued with patriotism and a sense of responsibility for the whole species. And it was by no means the case that we ignored the prob-lem of appealing to the rest of them. On the con-trary, we constantly discussed it as we studied the history of the Union. Yet there had already been so many failed attempts. What was the point of putting people on the rack and stretching them out to make them taller? When they didn't want it, and so all they could do was suffer. Once long ago, it had been foretold that a new man would be created, and that every cook would be capable of running the state. The state! And this at a time when even the smallest factory had been divided between those who gave orders and others who carried them out, cursing, stealing, and drinking in their spare time. The choice faced by our predecessors was inevitable. Yes, this meant propaganda. It wasn't possible to abandon appeals to hope, somehow trying to encourage them to take pride in their involvement, all the while writing off almost all this propaganda as a loss, as pure static or white noise that would never reach their ears. To light the fire of enthusiasm among them? How? Only if they felt shared responsibility. But they had no responsibility; nothing depended on them.

So our separateness—and even loneliness—

appeared to us as a necessary consequence of
our whole development, and of circumstances
in which the species was a hair's breadth away
from final extermination. It was our burden,
rather than a reason for pride, with the appropriate margin left over for error and chance, almost like a game of Russian roulette. Because
when they sent settlers out to Lakania nobody
questioned the principle that only men and
women with a solid preparation in the Union
were suitable, as this was supposedly the only
way to avoid the risk of infecting the new settlement with the disorder of ordinary people. Yet it
was clear that all this was an experiment—yet
another experiment—and that at least one experiment had not worked out very well, since
if everything had gone according to plan they
wouldn't have had to shut down Arguria. We
didn't know what had happened there. In general, I should point out that the Union is very different from what people imagine on the outside.
Since neither its internal organization nor what
goes on inside it are made public, a monolithic

image has arisen. In fact, everything depends on where you find yourself in the Union—in which section and on which floor. The structure is strictly hierarchical, and there is no communication between the branches and departments, only vertical communication of each department with the one above it.

Even before the expedition to Sardion, I pondered a great deal over our whole cause, though not with any real doubt. If I didn't share my thoughts with anybody, it was not because they seemed incompatible with my convictions, for they weren't. It was just that I hadn't been taught any language in which they could be expressed, so that they weren't so much thoughts as quarter-thoughts. Perhaps now I am distorting, ascribing greater insight to myself than I really had at the time. I guess I would describe it as follows: I was disquieted by the pressure of humanity on us, since we were supposed to be separate, but in reality we weren't entirely. Reason—which had scrutinized and created for millennia, from the first tools or the invention of fire—was incarnate in us, and we were its sole carriers, as we had not discovered any other rational beings in the galaxy. We vaunted not only our learning, but, above all, the rule of our reason over the passions and animal instinct, whether egoism or fear. And yet, when the struggle for survival abated, subsiding in the species thanks to universal protection from hunger, it seemed to shift over to us—to the Union. For the people on the outside were mistaken when they swallowed the intentionally disseminated legends about the filling of positions according to the verdicts of dispassionate computers. In reality, the whole Union was the scene of a struggle that was all the more fierce for being hidden under a multitude of pretenses, and the prize was power. That power, for its own sake—since nothing threatened us from below—obsessed us all, and I almost began to suspect that the inhabitants of Earth had been allowed to run wild and do as they pleased not simply because it would have been difficult to educate them. A passion had taken hold of our closed circle, preoccupying its members too completely for them to spare any energy for anything more than negative control of the crowds of others on the outside.

When they nominated me for a journey, I took it as an honorable distinction. Here, once again, the power of language endures, as certain words have preserved the tone they held for our most distant ancestors, even as we have become accustomed to giving them different meanings. For instance, despite all our knowledge, we still associate the word "journey" with separation and speed. You set off, and after however many hours you're somewhere else, as in the days when people journeyed by stagecoach or train, with traveling companions and shifting landscapes outside the window. Or when rockets lifted off from Earth, missiles launched by explosions. So against my will I connected travel with ideas like separation, moving away, and drawing near, while theoretically being prepared for the lack of anything of the kind. We should have abandoned the word "journey" the moment we broke through 90 percent of the speed of light;

and yet we still use it, just as we still use the word "speed." Our ship perhaps most resembled those old sailing vessels surrounded by the monotony of the ocean, becoming for their crews a kind of substitute earth, though admittedly we never had the sailing out from port, the waving of handkerchiefs, or the thunder of cannon in farewell, for the planet just vanished as if it had been blown away. Or perhaps the ship resembled a new country, from which there would be no return to the homeland, and instead of traveling companions we would have companions for life. Sardion is two and a bit light years away, and we would reach 99.5 percent of the speed of light, spending five of our own years away from Earth. Considering that the time difference jumps sharply at 99.5 percent, this meant that we wouldn't be returning to the same home planet. Five years on board our ship would amount to fifty years on Earth. This was the terrifying alienation of the Union from the mass of mortals. Upon our return, we could expect to meet some of our long-lived colleagues and friends, but otherwise we would find towering trees instead of saplings, children grown into old people, and nothing but memories of those who had once passed us by on city streets.

They do not send people on such expeditions without partners. And the Union takes great pains over their selection. Tolerance almost always verges upon contemptuous acquiescence, and in this way, too, the Union has isolated itself, looking indulgently upon polygamous habits among the masses, but demanding strict monogamy of its own. My wife, Ilen, went through the same training as I. In general, none of us ever dreamed of going near a woman outside the Union. We would have had too little in common. Between Ilen and myself there was complete understanding: we were bound by a common faith in the goal, and we could count on each other down to the similarity of all our instincts. And thus we were permitted to get married. They don't always give permission, only after long observation and favorable genetic calculations. So Ilen and I set off together with the

other couples of our crew for a time far removed
from that of our planet, and we were supposed
to return even closer to each other for our alienation from the earthly prisoners of another time
that was no longer ours.

In truth, I don't wish to go into the daily routine of those years. Duty, study, playing chess,
exercise, duty, study, and so on, over and over.
It wasn't very different from the routine in the
unit. Yet something is formed between people
trapped on board a ship, not just camaraderie or
friendship, mutual dislike or hatred, but a kalei-
doscopic system in constant creation and transformation. Only there, on the ship, did I sharply
experience the opposition between us, people,
and it, the indifferent universe. The shifting
system between us grew enormous, while the
worlds we passed grew small, as they were without speech. Yet the more I clung to this whirl-
ing of ourselves like planets spinning around one
another, the more I noticed my desire for something greater than what we were giving. What
did I desire? I didn't know. It was as if the ab-

sence of speech in the interplanetary void triggered a reinforcement or concentration of our
existence as warm-blooded and thinking beings
opposed to that void. I began to suspect that
the rumors about the reasons for the closure of
Arguria might have been true. Supposedly there
had been a revival of magic on the planet, and
a new hierarchy had arisen among the settlers,
turning the Union's order on its head, as they
gave their loyalty to self-appointed leaders of
collective shamanic rituals. It wasn't good news
that people with such talents had appeared, but,
assuming the rumors were not pure invention, I
could more or less understand where these temptations had come from. We had been trained to
admire the greatness of man. We—the vanguard
of the human race, sent farther than any before us—looked to one another for warmth and
comfort, and yet the system we had created was
based on a constant shuffling of petty ambitions,
complexes, and the impulse to dominate others.
In short, the barriers between "I" and "I" did
not disappear, but rather they grew, and I had

the feeling that I was touching a smooth surface, and that either something was hidden behind it or nothing at all—that perhaps human greatness was the cube root of nothing.

The specialized nature of our education didn't leave much room for many subjects beyond the history of technology. Still, I was conversant in the old imaginings about the planets, and especially about the Sun, the symbol of the greatest life-giving power: everything as a gift from the Sun; everything straining toward the Sun. We examined in some detail the views of a certain eighteenth-century European geologist, because he was a brilliant scientist, notwithstanding his religious doctrine, a sort of proto-Einstein, and because some of his scientific ideas turned out to be true. In treatises written in Latin, this strange eccentric wrote detailed accounts of journeys through heaven and hell, developing a comprehensive anthropocentric and heliocentric doctrine. In his works, there was nothing in the universe but God and man; even angels were redeemed human souls, while devils were the souls of the damned. And the whole of reality was twofold, existing both for itself and as a symbol of another, spiritual reality. The Sun was the highest symbol, representing God, and redeemed souls were to ascend ceaselessly from the lower sphere, which he called the lunar sphere, to the higher, solar sphere—ceaselessly, because the spiritual Sun was impenetrable and unfathomable, so that heaven was constant ascending movement. I must confess that as I recalled all this on the ship I envied those who still lived in their own solar system, with the Sun as their reference point. At our ship's speed, the Sun was eight minutes from Earth, and yet it was not the earthly Sun but other suns in other systems that the settlers would soon behold, and so I wondered whether man had strayed outside the circle inscribed by the very nature of his mind, whether he had lost his symbols, nourished in the earth and fed by the sun, moon, plants, and animals, so that our imagination didn't turn there, toward the trillions of heavenly bodies, but here, toward the other members of the crew, spinning around one another along our own individual orbits.

Our sojourn on Sardion. It's true that we were the first to take possession of the planet. Yet Sardion is just as the instruments sent there long ago showed it to be, and just as it appears on the screens. It deserves its name. During the months when we were building the station, I thought of the generations who would grow up there deprived of two colors, green and blue, surrounded only by the red of the rocks and the sky. Yellowy red, rusty red, purple red, grayish red, and a blackness somehow saturated with red. I won't recite the well-known facts about life-forms that undergo not evolution but involution. Certainly, what our eyes absorbed during that journey was astonishing, but we are adaptable. Long ago, the buildings of the great cities had astounded newcomers from the jungle, but they adapted rapidly, and soon learned even to drive cars. And I must say that nothing that happened during the journey could compare with the shock I experienced when I found myself back on Earth.

Now, as promised, it's time to return to my early youth, in a country so similar to this one that perhaps it's no coincidence that something drew me here. The same high mountains, forests, and lakes. My relatives, Wincenty and Felisa, lived all year round high up in a region that belonged at the time to the Botanists' Union. He was a biologist, specializing in fish. A very old house on a lake, out of which a river flowed—just like here. Except that the older houses there were built from cut stone. In winter—snow and skiers. In summer—a holiday paradise, with stables not far from the house, so that people could hire horses for mountain excursions. The whole thing took off to such an extent that every summer the horses had to be managed by Hauki, a young man who spent the winter off somewhere else on his studies—in other words, doing nothing. He would arrive as soon as the snows melted; he had his own room in the house, and he would stay until the fall.

I had barely emerged from childhood back then: I was at an awkward age. It seemed to me that I would never be like the others. I found various imagined deficiencies in my build, though in reality I was deficient in nothing. I would have been astonished if I had heard that anybody there regarded me as a handsome boy. My timidity and these various inhibitions were such that my physical talents remained dormant and uncoordinated. I adored Hauki, who for me was the inaccessible paragon of masculine harmony and nonchalant charm; whatever he touched was an effortless success, bowing before the ease with which he achieved it. In my opinion, nobody could compare with him. A muscular torso, long neck, small head, a face seemingly illuminated by big gray eyes, a straight, somewhat broad nose, high forehead, slightly frizzy chestnut hair—the ancient sculptors must have chosen such youths as their models for the gods. He went about naked to the waist, and I would gaze, completely enchanted, at the blue veins running down from his biceps to his wrists, which were wide and heavy. My adoration or even love was clearly not insignificant, since much later, on the ship, I was tormented by a single image, which seemed to contain the whole beauty of Earth: Hauki, as I had seen him for the first time, spurring his horse into a gallop, the most perfectly harmonious rhythm of steed and rider, the horse's nostrils and mane, the ripple of muscles, the contrast between the frozen human figure straining forward and the rush of the animal. Hauki regarded me with indulgent superiority; he barely noticed me, though sometimes, as he would correct my imperfect swimming style or explain my mistakes at horseback riding, I found a skeptically curious look in his eyes. In fact, we spent little time together, so I admired him mostly from afar. He was always busy, and always surrounded by his girls, who rightly belonged to him, and who rightly—as I humbly accepted—ignored me.

Wincenty was heavyset and good-hearted; he was learning to play the violin. Felisa mainly distinguished herself by the fact that she slaved away from morning till night, since the house and garden, and even partly the stables, rested on her shoulders. She dressed herself any old how, usually in black, in threadbare and ragged dresses, tying up her hair with a brightly colored kerchief. Those flowery green and yellow kerchiefs were the only proof that she might ever have used a mirror. She smothered Wincenty with tender care, but her general attitude to people was ironic—indeed, not just to people, but to life—her smirks and shrugs suggesting that one could expect nothing extraordinary from living, and that the only thing worth doing was to perform one's daily duties. As for me, she tried to replace my mother, taking care that I ate and changed my shirt, trying from time to time to draw me into conversation and somehow remedy my depression, because I was often sad and miserable. I clung to her, since I had nobody but them, and I sorely needed a little bit of warmth.

But why did Felisa come to my room one night, emboldening me to kiss her neck before opening her nightgown, under which she was naked? Why did she decide to initiate me into the affairs of love? Until then, I had thought of her not as a woman but simply as an older person, since at that age even a few years can seem like an enormous gulf. Did she simply feel sorry for a lonely adolescent whom she thought she could cheer up at such little cost? Had the boredom of her daily hustle and bustle become a burden to her? Or was it possible—though I didn't believe it—that there was somebody who saw a handsome boy in me after all? One way or another, the revelation I experienced fell upon me all the more suddenly for the fact that the same old Felisa, harried and preoccupied by her duties, turned out to be an entirely different being, and I couldn't comprehend how I could possibly have failed to see it. Her physical beauty cut right through me; for months, I walked about in a trance, screaming silently with rapture. Not that there had been any shortage of naked girls around me, but their all-too-obvious public nakedness was to Felisa's mysterious nakedness what the plump, common forms of pigeons or sparrows were to the flash of a wild bird in a thicket. If I sometimes felt guilty toward Wincenty, the feeling soon faded; I trusted her completely, and if she wished to bestow this gift upon me, then clearly this was how things were meant to be. I would never have presumed to judge her. Even if there were some ordinary polygamous instincts at play, almost on principle, greed didn't enter into it, for it wasn't Felisa's style just to snatch tasty morsels for herself. And later on, in the unit, when the recollection of certain details—looks and intonations—convinced me that Hauki couldn't have owed his place in the home to friendship alone, I still didn't judge her at all.

I'll leave it at that, for though my fate would carry me far away from those experiences—so far that even my shared identity with that timid adolescent seemed doubtful—on a much deeper level, under various layers, the memory was preserved, and it reemerged once I began to yearn for Earth onboard the ship. Trees, flowers, and mountain streams appeared to me shrouded in the spell of my first discovery, back then in my helpless and ridiculous youth. Perhaps they were even more beautiful, transformed and magnificent, because I had lost them forever. I hoped to see Earth again, but never the Earth evoked by that one extraordinary year. And, yes, I did eventually set foot on the grass again, the narrow green tongues bending in the breeze, and I heard the song of the cicadas. But the past was gone—both mine and other people's—and I found myself reeling, suddenly half an earthly century older, a traveler to an unknown land, to a civilization of people who were not my peers, and which I would have to learn anew.

I shouldn't have ventured beyond our circle, searching for the impossible. I met the familiar faces of Astronaut colleagues, and I held

the hand of Ilen, my contemporary. Yet the ob-
session that had begun on the ship forced me
to seek out continuity, perhaps even continuity with myself. I began a timid and round-
about search, convinced in advance of its futility. Then, an extraordinary thing happened:
I discovered that Wincenty and Felisa were still
alive, even living in the same house. I couldn't
bring myself to pick up the receiver, as I was
afraid to see their faces on the screen. I wrote
a letter. And before long, incredibly enough,
I held in my hands a quarto of paper covered
with pointy-lettered writing, even pointier than
before — Felisa's writing. She reported that although Wincenty had stopped working long
before, they had stayed in the old house, that
the water level of the lake had dropped and a
new biological station had been built, that their
health was poor — Wincenty could barely see
and walked with a cane — though somehow they
got by, that I was no doubt very busy, but that
since I had expressed my interest, for which they

were very grateful, they would be glad to see me once more before they died.

The longest section of the letter was devoted to answering my question about Hauki. As I had no doubt heard (I had not heard), Hauki had become an official at the United Bureaus, though he had suffered terribly, as the job had not interested him at all. Fortunately, he had found a suitable woman, and this had saved him. Here a name was mentioned, and I paused over it, for my memory connected the name with a vague figure, barely an outline, as when we try to reconstruct a dream upon waking. Hauki used to ride out with the very same girl on expeditions of several days, strapping rucksacks and sleeping bags to their saddles. In other words, I hadn't realized at the time that we were at such different stages. I saw Hauki as a carefree lord of life; in my immaturity, I could have no understanding of his seriousness or of his search for a permanent alliance with someone. They must have already sealed their union back then, making it lasting and final. A few years after my departure on the Sardion expedition, they had committed suicide together, and in the note left behind they wrote of a joint decision prompted by "the senselessness of everything."

My triumph. When a person envies, and I had envied Hauki, convinced that I could never compare with him . . . And now this was his failure. So I had won, not he. My strength, my skill, my mind. In the end, I had joined the elite, my image displayed with those of the other expedition members. I was still here— alive, young, and powerful—while nothing remained of Hauki, not even a handful of ashes, but merely a final trace in the memory of two elderly people. We can refuse to admit to ourselves that someone else's failure is our triumph, but once we have admitted it—and I have admitted it—something starts to happen inside us. I tried not to think about it, but my imagination kept connecting the small number of available images to reconstruct their gradual slide into despair, apathy, and grayness; I even imagined their conversations. I cannot precisely describe how my triumph—because it was shameful—turned to sorrow. Perhaps it was sorrow that all beauty is in vain. And then, for the first time in ages, the wave of my oscillator began to twitch; if I had been tested, I wouldn't have passed. My own victory appeared to me as unjustified, and I began to ask myself whether it might not have been more worthy of a human being to suffer defeat like them. In the end, their fate had been so much the worse as ours was better; as one scale went down, the other went up; the more faith in purpose and meaning for us, the less for them. So that suddenly I felt responsible for the misfortune of Hauki and others like him, for the whole order of things, though my rational mind still regarded this order as necessary.

Unfortunately, I went out there. My account of the visit will be awkward. The smallness, fragility, and fine-boned nature of our planet moved me, just as the charming weakness of a child is moving. But to find myself in a shrunken house, among familiar and shrunken appliances, and to

have it all before me as if inside a crystal ball
in the palm of my hand? And what is the testimony of our senses, our perception, if the same
table, the same door frame, the same threshold
can be one thing, and then later something else
entirely? Except that at least the table and the
threshold had remained the same, while it was
I who had changed. Admittedly, I didn't recognize the pines around the house, and I got lost in
the altered distances of the hillside, overgrown
with new forest. But I would prefer not to speak
of the actual moment of meeting them. One
recognizes and does not recognize—pure terror.
This faded, blind, shrunken human relic was the
athletic and broad-shouldered Wincenty. This
gray, shriveled old woman had once been my
Felisa. A multitude of vertical wrinkles had con-
tracted and obliterated her mouth; her teeth had
slid forward, exposed from the gums, and it was
they—not her faded eyes—that now dominated
her face, or rather her skull, which was ready to
dispense with the remains of its muscles, petrify-

ing inside the parchment of skin that was stuck to it.

I pronounced the word: sorrow. But perhaps it doesn't fit, since I want to convey a feeling for which words haven't yet been invented. Just as things that were once large had become small, so it was with desires, passions, betrayals, and faults—all reduced to miniature dimensions, their wretchedness crying out only for forgiveness. Not that some human being should forgive. There is almost a need for a kind of universal principle, a deity, which could do nothing but forgive, which could take no offense at humans, since they are so poor and impermanent. They are not even this, for they cannot stop anything. Where was the real Felisa? Was she the one with the olive-scented skin from the song of love, or the one who stood before me now? On the sofa, whose dark wood was the same shade as long before, I recognized the checkered pattern, and its familiar design humiliated me. Even a thing that seemed so easily destructible could resist time,

but not they, dependent on the pulsing of weary-
ing hearts.

In the transformation that has taken place in
me since that moment, what I have learned has
helped me very little. I may have learned to dis-
dain chaos, but now I had that chaos inside me,
and it forced me to test my habits. What was
the point of armor or a corset if it did not cover
weakness? Perhaps we were similar to our ancestors, whose fear of the flaw inside them had
made them line up in cohorts and follow orders,
deluding themselves that the flaw in each of them
would disappear when they marched together.
Previously it had concerned me that we were not
sufficiently pure or sufficiently removed from
disordered and foolishly excitable humanity, but
now those knightly or soldierly commandments
of mine seemed to have lost their justification.
In any case, this was surely not a matter of two
separate accusations but rather the continuation
of the same vague anxiety—in other words, I
had never been a perfect Astronaut. The nature
of my slow and gradual transformation is still

not entirely clear to me today. The main thing was probably the appearance of a single growing desire: to lose. This dark, goading compulsion would not cease to torment me until I fulfilled its demands. It was as if solidarity with them—with people—was pushing me toward the edge, and I could be with them only by falling.

Here I should add that my marriage to Ilen, instead of protecting me, only contributed further to my transformation. I looked at her as if into a mirror, while she continued imperturbably to be what I had ceased to be. Her virtues seemed to be made of glass, her insides washed out and transparent, when in truth the inside of a person is always unclean. She took pleasure in our return to Earth, in sports and entertainments, and I accompanied her, though more and more I kept silent. My condition worried her, but I didn't want to infect anybody with my disease, or convert anybody, least of all her. The infirmity was mine, and mine alone. So our marriage had been consecrated, as we were contemporaries, but I was being dragged back down to that poorer earth, where there was nothing but fear and loneliness.

If human life was what it was, then it meant to lose. As if, by meeting the fate shared by all, one could reproach some unknown power, shaming or provoking it. If it destroyed people with such indifference, then so much the worse for it. Like Hauki, I simply felt "the senselessness of it all." You might call it a desire for death. But no, I consented only to the sands trickling through the hourglass, to the inner turmoil that artificially cultivated virtues could never conceal, to the thoughtlessness of the young Felisa, to the shared lot of the children of Adam. I wasn't completely without hope. Until then, I had lived superficially, but now the time had come for meditation and wandering, in the expectation that things always become clearer when we remove the screen, suddenly exposing ourselves to time, which dismantles us piece by piece, so that we might be prepared for an abrupt end, better prepared than the Astronauts on their expeditions, who do not have to fear the HBN.

I disappeared, without warning anybody, not even Ilen. I changed my name. Our longevity requires twelve procedures a year—one per month—and I've been out of the Union for two years now, so the job has been done. If they find me, I will no longer be one of them. I don't regret it. I have been wandering and studying the Earth, while my flaw—my weakness—has become ever more apparent. Of course, it wasn't easy just to abandon Ilen like that, but what use was my rebellion to her? Flawless and cheerful, she will write me off as a dead loss, faithful to the cause, and when I'm long gone, she will join new expeditions, forever young. And if it happened that she met me again as an old man, I doubt that it would bother her. I say I don't regret it, since for me it all began with Hauki's defeat, but now I think that if the whole human species had the choice either of losing or winning as we have won, then winning wouldn't be worth it.

Appendix
Ephraim's Liturgy
Czeslaw Milosz

PART ONE: COMMENTARY
EXPLAINING WHO EPHRAIM WAS

It all happened in times when human anxiety was less hidden than ever before, as the multitude of activities to which so much time and energy had once been devoted had revealed their futility and uselessness. It was with a certain astonishment that people attempted to reconstruct the course of that earlier transformation, all the more distant in time as even the period it had inaugurated was clearly coming to an end. Of course, theoretically, people understood why the ancestors, shaken in their customs by the Age of Reason and searching for surrogate cults, had gradually come to worship the humblest of occupations, so that the petty and insignificant became great and significant, only now to shrink back down to its proper dimensions. Yet theoretical knowledge—backed by computerized linguistic analysis of the prevailing mentality of a given month or year—could never fully explain the riddle of the honors and privileges awarded for the playing of the lute, the writing of sonnets, or the coating of wood or canvas with paint. For millennia, man had taken pleasure in the products of his hand and mind, delighting in the tangible proof of his versatile talents, but it had never occurred to him that what he created might be called Art, or that it merited idolatrous worship. So how, people asked, and when, had the breakthrough occurred? Indeed, it was a breakthrough of no small import, for it had added yet another division to the countless divisions of people into opposing categories: namely, a division between higher minds, capable of penetrating literature and art, and lower minds, condemned to crude and unrefined amusements.

The decline of a set of views that had been adopted more or less automatically over the lengthy course of the whole period was made inevitable by sheer weight of numbers. In the middle of the nineteenth century, painters and poets were regarded as somewhat inferior persons of dubious mental health. They formed little groups of so-called bohemians, lamenting their low social status and speaking contemptuously of their well-fed fellow citizens, describing them as everymen, philistines, and even as swine. As for the novelists, they diligently toiled away in the hopes of providing the public with interesting tales, though certain individuals among them began to reveal greater pretensions and ambitions, spending weeks on a single page of prose, while convincing themselves that their martyr's self-discipline had some higher meaning inaccessible to ordinary people. At the same time, the snobbism of the moneyed classes offered a glimpse of the future, when the art galleries and libraries, often built in the midst of sprawling parks, would be seen as temples of civilization.

By the middle of the twentieth century, the number of artists, sculptors, poets, and prose writers reached into the hundreds of thousands. From then on, it would grow exponentially, partly as a result of the technological accelera-

tion that would deprive the masses of any influence on political and economic decisions, while
guaranteeing, to whoever wanted it, a small in-
come with no obligation actually to work, thanks
to automation. This circumstance merely en-
couraged the spontaneous development of a
phenomenon that had arisen for other reasons,
but it also explains why at the beginning of the
next century there were millions of individuals officially registered as "people of the arts,"
a category that included jugglers, magicians
pulling rabbits out of hats, tightrope walkers,
and makers of moving images projected onto
screens. In any case, the figures are unreliable,
since millions of others — unrecorded by statistics — devoted themselves to molding sculptures
from glass and metal, writing poems and novels,
and mixing paints on palettes. Even more tell-
ing are the tacitly accepted moral taboos of the
time. While the most dubious slogans, including the propagation of suicide and child murder, met with benevolent indulgence, and the
most vulgar sexual eccentricities offended no-

body, the prohibition against blasphemy refused to go away. Those who committed it soon confronted faces pale with horror, discovering that they had effectively excluded themselves from human society. All it took was to say that art was just a game, or a mere display of technical skill, or that it was wrong to find the revelation of elusive mysteries in its productions. After all, the libraries were mostly stocked with microfilmed books about these mysteries (which, as we have seen, included the pulling of rabbits out of hats), together with more books about these books.

The existence of such an extraordinary multitude had to have its consequences. In earlier times, much had been written about "creators" and "consumers," but now these expressions had become completely obsolete, since only "creators" remained—that is, if we exclude that portion of the human species preferring to busy itself exclusively with money-making, sex, or underwater hunting. It was like an enormous hall filled with endless rows of pianos. Everybody was playing his own instrument, straining to drown out the others, and even if he were to have stopped playing for a brief moment, he would have heard only his immediate neighbor in the general din. The ridiculousness of this activity—which was meant to be aristocratic, but had become common—dismayed the more discriminating. Meanwhile, other factors were preparing the way for a sudden crash. To find the first symptoms of the declining faith in art, we must cast back to the years when so-called structuralism came into vogue, joyfully adopted for a time by those who were both creators and commentators, as it seemed to confirm the sense of their own gravity and grandeur. Unfortunately, while each of them had hoped to save himself from oblivion by committing his name to a book or to the corner of a painting, structuralism heralded the frustration of this aim. For structuralism taught that it was not they who used language, but language that used them, not they who created style, but style that created them, so that all baroque sonnets became one sonnet written by the baroque *episteme*, and all baroque paintings were one painting, a teaching that clearly applied to the present as well, undermining their confidence in the supposedly unique and individual qualities of whatever they produced. Structuralism was made to the measure of the new era, where 100,000 almost identical poems appeared in print every day, and 100,000 almost identical products of the so-called fine arts were exhibited to the public.

The all-too-serious needs of the human heart expressed themselves in the cult of art, hoping that the death of the myth would not leave a terrifying void behind it. Those disappointed could not have been expected to find consolation in philosophy. Their training in hazy visions, waking dreams, half-tones, and allusions to nonexistent depths was too one-sided, while almost nobody had a philosophical education, since what the schools and universities taught as philosophy was scarcely fit for consumption. Only mathematicians and physicists ventured into those columned rooms, where marble busts of Descartes, Kant, and Husserl presided over debates on the philosophy of the data of consciousness, or, more often, on the philosophy of language. Once it had been pushed aside into the role of servant to the exact sciences, the friend of wisdom—as philosophy had once been known—could no longer promise any wisdom at all. Ordinary people perceived a world reduced to a mere function of the mind as a pale, unreal, and repulsive one; consequently, just as their bodies rejected unhealthy food, they refused to assimilate a knowledge that seemed to degrade reality. Undoubtedly, people still yearned for a philosophy of being, but there was no longer any such thing. Theologians had so thoroughly blocked its potential with Thomas Aquinas that it had proven impossible to unblock, despite a few brilliant attempts from the Catholic representatives of realism. Meanwhile, Marxism continued to pay the price for its eschatological prophecies of man's freedom from alienation, which had met with total failure, since the universality of art was simply a result of the process of alienation on a massive scale. Although Marxism strove for

a long time to cover up its ontological meager-
ness with various borrowings, mainly from the
French Romantic poet Teilhard de Chardin,
these attempts were never successful. It was no
surprise that such conditions led to the spread of
another class of wisdom, which did not even call
itself philosophy—a fluid, vague, and indefinite
wisdom, calling to mind the tangled menageries
of half-animal, half-divine beings that adorned
the great architectural edifices in the jungles of
southern Asia. In any case, its origins clearly
suggested this region, and while the mission-
ary journeys of various gurus from India were
nothing new, they had never before attracted so
many disciples and adherents. For more critical
minds, it was a sham wisdom, a parasitic growth
thriving on the generally poor state of education
and the habits instilled by mental chaos.

This was the historical background to
Ephraim's activities. He himself was far from
an eremite like his patron, Saint Ephraim the
Syrian, though the times in which he lived were
not entirely unlike those of the Council of Nicaea.

From his earliest youth, Ephraim had found himself among a cacophonous mélange of races, languages, and traditions, in a great bouillabaisse of
civilizations, and he was whirled around by its
eddying movement like all his contemporaries,
most of whom were the homeless descendants
of the Christian churches and the synagogue,
further deprived even of the surrogate religious
consolations that art had temporarily supplied.
He encountered a multitude of sects and frater-
nities, serving as shelters and sources of passable
warmth for an atomized humanity, and he met
more than one of their founders, yoga masters,
magicians, and charlatans. The old chemical
preparations, taken collectively for the purposes
of spiritual elevation, still found stubborn con-
servative supporters, who ran countless meditation houses and Timothy Leary Institutes, but
the convenient electro-exciters were much more
popular, as the flow of current to the nerve cen-
ters in the brain could be regulated, so that cosmic bliss came without the transitional stages
of diabolical torment that accompanied almost

all the synthetic imitations of peyote. Although moral and legal acceptance had taken away much of the charm of the so-called sex orgies, they had not disappeared, and their participants insisted that this was still the most effective way to experience what a long-forgotten philosopher had once termed the Metaphysical Feeling of the Strangeness of Existence. Admittedly, all these pursuits remained on a rather folkish level, while the more intellectually active were interested primarily in religion. Yet here they hit upon certain difficulties. The era inaugurated by the Reformation and the Protestant churches — with their later cultivation of the "death of God" theology over the course of many decades — had come to an end. Since then, the churches had steadily dissolved, supplying adepts for the new Buddhist monasteries. As a result of its different civilizational foundations, this western Buddhism represented less a religion than a form of the hazy eastern wisdom we have already discussed. Religion meant the combined Roman and Orthodox churches. Yet the very type of imagination shared by the people of the time formed an almost insurmountable barrier— whether or not they desired to believe—so that even the most ardent among them were lost somewhere on the border between Christianity and agnosticism.

Ephraim had drawn certain conclusions from the collapse of the myth of art. For there was much to ponder: the doctrine of "correspon- dences," once stolen from Emmanuel Sweden- borg, had served poets and their disciples, rhetoricians and grammarians, in defense of the symbolic code that permitted human beings to communicate their moments of illumination— their brushes with the impenetrable core of being—to one another. The whole movement that gave birth to abstract art over the course of 150 years ultimately reduced itself to this prin- ciple in various forms. Yet the promise of com- munication led to its negation, raising a Tower of Babel in the hubbub of pianos clamoring to drown one another out. If the scriptures of the Old and New Testaments remained the only fully formed voice of man, in spite of all the efforts of this crowd of talents and geniuses, then one had to acknowledge that divinity had penetrated humanity only once, and that the fundamental error of art was the error of all surrogates. Perhaps Ephraim would not have been so harsh had he not observed at such close quarters the miracle workers prescribing their chemical and electric "shortcuts" to the inexpressible, and had he not even taken part in some of these experiments in his youth. The connection between these "shortcuts" and the dreams of artists was beyond doubt to him. After all, had the poets not been the first to discover the "artificial paradises" of hashish and opium back in the age of steam and gas lamps, thus revealing what they were truly striving toward—for instance, as one of them put it, "through the disorganization of all the senses"? Ephraim was neither a philosopher nor a theologian. He wished to communicate with others beyond a domain that had been thoroughly compromised, even if the fanatics of aesthetic experience still defended it here and there. He resisted the silence that had been imposed on all by the disintegration of speech into mere sounds, mutterings, and shrieks. The presence of men and women gathered together to experience their own fragility and impermanence in time—their humanity—was crucially significant, but it was necessary to put speech into their mouths, and that speech could be imparted only by ritual. From the moment of the abolition of Latin, the Catholic liturgy had turned increasingly toward the remnants of local folk traditions, which had retained their simple and comprehensible language, until finally Negro spirituals came to form the very foundation of the ceremony. Without denying the merits of this genre, Ephraim—who understood his own craft as an ability to shape readymade material, just as the painters of icons had once done—turned to forgotten liturgical texts in Latin and Old Church Slavonic, as well as to the Bible. The thinking of his patron, author of hymns and homilies, was apparently not without influence on his intentions. "The History of

Ephraim, Deacon of Edessa," preserved in the manuscript of Palladius's "Paradise," tells of a dream that Ephraim the Syrian once had in his youth, before he had written any of his numerous works. He dreamed that a vine heavy with grapes grew from his mouth, and great flocks of birds swooped down upon them, but the more they ate, the more numerous and abundant the grapes became.

If Ephraim entertained any hope that he might help somebody, then we can imagine that this hope must have been modest, as he showed a good sense of the moderation appropriate to his time. He was active within his own community or congregation, which did not differ in any fundamental way from similar spontaneously arising groups, all of which were loosely associated with one another, a circumstance made possible by the blurring of divisions between believers and nonbelievers, as they had once been known, and by the decision of the Church to relinquish all administrative control—in short, the changes delivered by the First Council of Jerusalem. Since mass appeal and universality were synonymous with degradation and contamination, nobody was keen to share with other groups the forms of ritual they had invented for themselves. Accordingly, the variations introduced by Ephraim—for instance, the sermon in rhythmical speech and the confession as a kind of therapy session with the whole congregation instead of a doctor or priest—were the property of a single group, and remained unknown outside it. We publish them here for the first time, drawing on the extant notes and recordings.

DEACON: I go to the altar of my God.

CONGREGATION: To the God who makes joyful
            my youth.

DEACON: Judge me and put not my case with
            the case of the godless.

            Let not the debased and cunning
            man have power over me.

CONGR.:   You are my strength; why have you
            spurned me?

            Why do I walk the earth in sor-
            row, while my enemy remains with
            me day and night?

DEACON: Send light and truth, for they shall
            lead me to your mountain, to your
            sacred home.

CONGR.:   I go to the altar of my God, to the
            God who makes joyful my youth.

DEACON: I shall praise you on the zither, for
            you are my God. Why does my sor-

row cease not and why do I live with
the fear of death?

CONGR.: Lay your hope in God, for time shall
be fulfilled and you shall praise him
in the glory of your body.

DEACON: I go to the altar of my God.

CONGR.: To the God who makes joyful my
youth.

DEACON: I call to him and he comes to my
aid.

CONGR.: He who created heaven and earth.

DEACON: Before him, my God, I confess.

CONGR.: May God almighty have mercy
upon you and heeding not your
errors lead you into eternal life.

DEACON: Amen.

CONGR.: I confess before God almighty and
before those who died long ago yet
still live and hear me, whatsoever
were their names—Mary, Peter,
John, Paul—before all their holy
congregation, and before you, my
brother, that I have erred greatly in

thought, word, and deed. Through my fault, through my fault, through my most grievous fault.

Therefore I ask the people here with me, Mary, Peter, John, Paul, and all their holy congregation, and also you, my brother, to pray for me to the Lord of heaven and earth, our God.

DEACON: May God almighty have mercy upon you and heeding not your errors lead you into eternal life.

CONGR.: Amen.

DEACON: May our hidden, merciful, and almighty God show us his mildness, his goodness and his forgiveness of sins.

CONGR.: Amen.

DEACON: You shall not hide yourself from us and you shall restore us to life.

CONGR.: And your people shall be joyful in you.

DEACON: Let us come to know your mercy.

CONGR.:   And give us faith in salvation through you.

DEACON: Hear my prayer.

CONGR.:   And let my cry come to you.

DEACON: Take us away, we beseech you O Lord, from our iniquities, that we might become worthy to accept the words of your mysteries with pure mind.

Through our oneness with your son Jesus. Amen.

Through the good deeds of those whose hands have touched this stone and of all who love you, send forth my sins into oblivion. Amen.

Here I lay you into the flame; may you find the blessing of him in whose name you shall burn.

Peace be with you.

CONGR.:   And with your spirit.

Lesson (Ecclesiastes 12: 1-8)

[1]Remember also your Creator in the days of your youth, before the evil days come, and the years draw nigh, when you will say, "I have no pleasure in them";

[2]before the sun and the light and the moon and the stars are darkened and the clouds return after the rain,

[3]in the day when the keepers of the house tremble, and the strong men are bent, and the grinders cease because they are few, and those that look through the windows are dimmed,

[4]and the doors on the street are shut; when the sound of the grinding is low, and one rises up at the voice of a bird, and all the daughters of song are brought low;

[5]they are afraid also of what is high, and terrors are in the way; the almond tree blossoms, the grasshopper drags itself along and desire fails, because man goes to his eternal home, and the mourners go about the streets;

[6]before the silver cord is snapped, or the golden bowl is broken, or the pitcher is broken at the

fountain, or the wheel broken at the cistern, [7]and the dust returns to the earth as it was, and the spirit returns to God who gave it.

[8]Vanity of vanities, says the Preacher; all is vanity.

CONGR.:   In you, O Lord, have we abided from generation to generation.

DEACON: As you cleansed the lips of the prophet Isaiah with a burning coal, may you cleanse my heart and my lips, almighty God, so that I may become worthy to proclaim your good news. Through Jesus your anointed one, our Lord. Amen.

              Peace be with you.

CONGR.:   And with your spirit.

Gospel (Matthew 21: 18–22)

[18]In the morning, as he was returning to the city, he was hungry. [19]And seeing a fig tree by the wayside he went to it, and found nothing on it but leaves only. And he said to it, "May no fruit ever come from you again!" And the fig tree with-

ered at once. [20]When the disciples saw it, they marveled, saying, "How did the fig tree wither at once?" [21]And Jesus answered them, "Truly, I say to you, if you have faith and never doubt, you will not only do what has been done to the fig tree, but even if you say to this mountain, 'Be taken up and cast into the sea,' it will be done. [22]And whatever you ask in prayer, you will receive, if you have faith."

Sermon

He was hungry. That, brothers and sisters, is all
    we can understand
when we ponder, and I know that each one of
    you must ponder,
upon this extraordinary meeting of our
    congregation here.
For you and you and I repeat the words to
    ourselves: I am,
I am here. My hand, my knee, my face, so
    familiar to the touch,
my face, from reflections in mirrors and the
    eyes of other people.

My hunger, my bodily greed, my tears, my
  weariness.
And yet—how is it possible?—we come
  together to say "we,"
recognizing ourselves in others. Oh, among all
  the world's riddles,
this one torments us most: the particular and
  the general.
For is not each of us here the one and only to
  himself,
desiring the other only insofar as the other
  might pay homage to him,
strengthening him in his ambition, bestowing
  gifts and tending to him?
Is not each of us the one and only truly called
  to exist?
So whence this word "we," brothers and sisters?

He was hungry. Only in the most simple and
  elementary things
do we recognize ourselves. For who can truly
  be certain

that another person has ever known joy or
    sorrow?
Only in hunger and in thirst, our common
    infancy.
He became angry, like a child unable to
    comprehend
that there are laws for things, just as we rebel
    every day
against the immutable order of cause and effect
that turns our dreams about ourselves into
    nothing.
Yet the fig tree has withered. A childish victory,
a divine victory! And so the child is elevated,
and so our own naïve power is acknowledged.
We exist under an iron law: what lives must die,
what would exist alone is sealed in a number,
vanishing into millennia, into billions of
    billions.
Yet the fig tree has withered. Can you hear the
    cry of the disciples,
who have seen and touched, and yet can
    scarcely believe?

*   *   *

Why did he punish the tree? Had it wronged
    him in some way?
After all, we love trees, treating them with
    veneration,
ever awaiting encounters with playful dryads,
and we are sorry when their green leaves curl
    and crackle in the fire.
But Nature will not save us. We know this full
    well,
though we still find longing and memory in
    her.

From beyond Nature, he came to call us
to participate in the power of the same prayer.
And what does it matter, brothers and sisters,
    that our faith is weak,
neither moving mountains nor saving us from
    death,
when we have been given a sign, a vision of our
    true essence
in the first glimpse of the unaccomplished
    kingdom?

*   *   *

As we gather here today, separate and yet one,
so shall we commune when time and space
  meet their end.
Let no number pollute our hand or head,
for every particular being will find
  confirmation. Amen.

CONGR.:   I have risen and I am always with
            you. Alleluia.

                You have laid your hand upon
            me. Alleluia.

                High and wondrous is your
            knowledge. Alleluia. Alleluia.

                You have searched me and before
            I open my lips

                you know what word I shall utter.
            Alleluia.

DEACON: Where shall I go from your spirit?
                Or where shall I flee from your
            presence?
CONGR.:   If I ascend to heaven, you are there!

If I make my bed in Sheol, you
are there!

DEACON: If I take the wings of the morning
   and settle at the farthest limits of
the sea,

CONGR.:   Even there your hand shall lead me,
   and your right hand shall hold
me fast.

DEACON: If I say, "Surely the darkness shall
cover me,
   and the light about me become
night,"

CONGR.:   Even the darkness is not dark to you;
   the night is bright as the day,
   for darkness is as light to you.

DEACON: For it was you who formed my in-
ward parts;
   you knit me together in my
mother's womb.

CONGR.:   I praise you, for I am fearfully and
wonderfully made.
   Wonderful are your works;
   that I know very well.

DEACON: My frame was not hidden from you,
        when I was being made in secret,
        intricately woven in the depths of
the earth.

CONGR.:   Your eyes beheld my unformed substance.
        In your book were written
        all the days that were formed for
me,
        when none of them as yet existed.

DEACON: How weighty to me are your
thoughts, O God!
        How vast is the sum of them!

CONGR.:   I try to count them—they are more
than the sand.
        I come to the end—I am still with
you.

DEACON: The kingdom is yours for ever and
ever. Alleluia.

CONGR.:   The dominion is yours from generation to generation. Alleluia.

CZESLAW MILOSZ (1911–2004) was a Polish poet, novelist, essayist, translator, and diplomat of Polish and Lithuanian descent who defected to the West in 1951. His 1953 book *The Captive Mind* is a classic text on totalitarianism. Milosz was professor of Slavic languages and literatures at the University of California, Berkeley, for more than thirty years. In 1980 he was awarded the Nobel Prize in Literature and was also the recipient of the Neustadt International Prize for Literature and the U.S. National Medal of Arts.

STANLEY BILL is a lecturer in Polish Studies at the University of Cambridge.